I0691387

The Toy

First Edition

Published by The Nazca Plains Corporation
Las Vegas, Nevada
2009

ISBN: 978-1-935509-12-7

Published by

The Nazca Plains Corporation ®
4640 Paradise Rd, Suite 141
Las Vegas NV 89109-8000

PUBLISHER'S NOTE
The Toy is a work of fiction created wholly by *Pete Brown's* imagination. All characters are fictional and any resemblance to any persons living or deceased is purely by accident. No portion of this book reflects any real person or events.

Cover, Russell Duparcq and Lou Oates
Art Director, Blake Stephens

The Toy

First Edition

Pete Brown

Part 1

It was those "three strikes and you're out" laws that did it for me. I've always been a bit of a rebel, and always wanted a good night out and a bit of fun. It's just that sometimes I went a bit wild. After the firs time we did a bit of damage to a bar I should have listened to my buddies and calmed down a bit, I guess. I suppose I liked going to bars because there was not much else to do in the small, isolated town there in the plains – most of my buddies got married soon after they left high school, but somehow that passed me by – I had a lot of girl friends, of course, but just never got around to popping the question. Now, at 28, the opportunity just isn't there – all the girls are married, and when I want a fuck, it's a question of hanging around in the bars and seeing if anything turns up. There are always a few semi-itinerant waitresses who want a night in the sack every now and then with a stud, and I'm always there to oblige.

Anyway, as I was saying, it was the "three strikes" thing that got me. After the first time our evening went too far and we did some damage, I got a couple of nights in the local jail to "cool off," as the sheriff said, but it did go on my record. I also now see that I was hasty in starting a brawl with the guy from out of town who damaged my car when he shot a light – the only light in town, in fact. He was some fancy lawyer on vacation in the area, and of course he insisted on pressing charges. I got two months in the County Jail for that, and, to add insult to injury, I even had to pay for the damage to his car when it was not even my fault in the first place.

Don't get me wrong – I'm not violent or hot-headed, or anything. I work hard, very hard, labouring in construction, and that leaves me pretty exhausted most evenings. It also gives me hard, strong muscles of course, as there's still a lot of "grunt" work to be done on a site. In fact, given the amount of machinery in use, you'd be surprised how much carrying, digging, and general sheer physical work still goes on – and it's guys like me that get to do it. Most of the drivers of those big sophisticated machines have some education – they need it, else the owners can't get insurance. That means that the work that's left over no longer gets shared around – all of it falls on the few guys like me who can't find any other work to do in a small town like ours. I've often thought of moving away, but it's not easy when you've lived somewhere all your life and have no education. If I went to one of the big cities I don't suppose that the money I would make would be enough to give me the things I can have out here in the boonies – at least I have a car, and can afford a small place of my own so I have a bit of privacy when one of those waitresses does come my way!

It's one of those women that really did it for me. I'd foolishly broken my usual resolution and had let her stay three nights with me – I usually like to "fuck and go" with these ladies, as I don't want them clinging to me. But this one, well, I don't know – we might have had something a bit more, I suppose. We were great together in bed, and she had a sort of cute smile and a nice way of talking. She was terrified of her husband finding her, though, and although she would never talk about it, I guessed her marriage must have been pretty rough. We were actually in the sack together when the door of my place was kicked open and this guy was standing there with a gun. She screamed, because it was hubby who had tracked her down, and from the way he was shouting at her it looked pretty serious. Even though I was stark naked, I thought I had to do something, as the way things were going I just knew he would shoot both of us.

As he stood over the woman screaming obscenities at her, his attention wandered and I launched myself at him – not easy, when you're lying in the bed, but if you're really fit like me, it's surprising what you can do, especially when your life is threatened! I felt the buttons on his shirt and the buckle on his belt scrape all along my naked body as I hurled myself at him. Then we struggled, and there were shots. It's not like you see on the TV – when a gun goes off in your bedroom, the sound is overwhelming – it almost deafens you.

I knew the place was getting pretty trashed as we skirmished around, but then I felt his body suddenly relax as we continued to grapple. I realised he was no longer resisting, and gradually got to my feet. There was blood everywhere – one of his shots had killed the woman, and somehow, as we struggled, he'd managed to shoot himself. Honest!

Well, I knew I was innocent. But when the sheriff came and found two bodies, and me, totally naked but covered in blood, he just arrested me. It was of course stupid of me to pick up the gun where it had fallen from his hands, and that was what finally convicted me – the jury simply didn't believe my story. Faced with two bodies, and with my record of brawling and so on, they decided I was probably mostly at fault. Although it was only a "murder two" rap, and I might have got away with ten years, the "three strikes" thing automatically bumped me to whole life, with no prospect of parole.

Actually, after the first few days, the State Prison turned out not to be so bad. I've told you that I'm a tough guy physically, and my size anyway makes me look pretty intimidating – I'm 6'4" in my bare feet, and everything else is in proportion. So with my record of shooting and brawling, it didn't even trouble me to think that one of the other cons might try to turn me into some guy's bitch. At least in that respect I had nothing to worry about as I was locked into my cell on the first night. Of course it took some getting used to hearing my cell mates jerking off –

with four of us in such a small space you just can't help hearing another guy beating his meat, and after trying to do it ever so quietly myself, I gave up and just jerked myself off as usual. One hundred percent of guys jerk off, after all, so there's no shame in it – you just don't talk about it to the other guys or even acknowledge that they're doing it.

I spent most of my time in the gym – it helps you to keep sane. My already tough, hard body got even more defined in the next few months. I've never been a great one for reading or anything, and you get tired of talking to the other guys as there's nothing new to say after a while. But you can always work out, and it leaves you relaxed and ready for the sack if you do it hard enough. I suppose I hoped that one day I might get out, but the guards used to almost enjoy reminding me that I was there for ever, and I got to believing that it must be true. The lawyer I'd had at the last trial came and visited me once or twice, and even though he tried to sound enthusiastic and cheerful and told me how he was appealing my case and trying to get public support for me, I could tell that he didn't really believe there was any chance at all.

A few years back I know that the appeals process could drag on for years, but along with the very tough "three strikes" laws the country had passed the so-called "speedy justice" provisions, so after only six months there I finally knew I was there for ever when the Supreme Court finally refused to even reconsider my case. They said that my trial had been properly conducted, and that the jury had taken a view they were entitled to form of my general character, so that the balance of probability was that I had done the shooting.

I suppose I should have been in despair, but what's the point? What you can't change, you may as well learn to live with. There was a different prison regime, however, and as one of the new class of "whole life, no hope" prisoners I was in a special category – the prison service was worried about us guys, as with no hope of ever getting out it was thought that we might see no problem in attacking the guards. I was therefore shipped to the new maximum security prison on the other side of the state, and joined several hundred other men who, like me, were there for ever.

To be fair, they made it as good as they could. We had a lot of "freedom" inside the prison walls, and were not locked in cells all the time. There was a lot of recreation facilities, a good gym, basketball court, library, and all that stuff. We rarely saw guards, and provided we behaved, we were mostly left to ourselves. It seemed that, providing there was no trouble, the authorities were prepared to mostly let the prisoners mostly run things for themselves and they only intervened if there were major disturbances. It sickened me, actually, to see how some of the weaker and younger guys were picked on by the tougher men – although I wasn't going to do anything about it, as a guy has to learn to look after himself, or take the consequences. But each time there was "fresh meat" shipped in, I would lie awake and hear the screams as they were introduced to their new role as a gang-leader's fuck toy. I had nothing to worry about of course, with my physique and reputation ensuring that I was left well alone. I suppose I could have picked one of those cute guys for my own pleasure, but I never fancied guys' asses – I just carried on as I'd mostly done all my life, beating my meat before I went to sleep.

We got used to seeing parties of "suits" being shown around by the governor. Our State was a pioneer in making these prisons which were virtually escape-proof but "self governing," and it seemed the whole world wanted to come and observe how it was going. I was working out as usual in the one day gym when just such a party came past, and as I was well into my routines I was covered in sweat – I usually took my T-shirt off when I was not on the weight machines, to try to keep it clean. I was just pounding away on the treadmill doing my daily eight miles wearing just my running shorts when they came in. It was kind of interesting, as these visitors were obviously foreigners – they had interpreters with them, and some of them were in Arab dress.

I ignored them, of course, and just kept on running. But the governor finally told one of the guards to make me stop, and I was brought over and made to stand in front of the party of visitors. "See," I heard the governor say, "This is a typical prisoner. He knows he'll never leave here, but he still finds it worthwhile to keep in good shape. We find that providing we do provide opportunities for exercise and so on, there's a lot less tension in the place. I felt pretty foolish, actually, standing there with my chest heaving and the sweat running off me. I could feel the silky fibre of my running shorts clinging to me, and it was almost as if I was some sort of animal, the way the visitors were looking at me. In particular, one of the Arabs was paying very close attention to me, and his eyes raked up and down my body as I stood there. He stepped forward, and I thought he was going to start actually feeling my muscles, but the governor cautioned him back, saying that prisoners could, after all, be violent.

I thought no more about his incident, actually, except that about a month later I was called into the governor's office. There was a guy of about my own age in there with him, dressed in what looked like an expensive suit.

"Is this the man?" the governor asked him as I came in.

"Yes. This is the one we identified, from the surveillance tapes. Will you be so good as to leave us alone now, please, governor?"

To my amazement, as the governor was "God" in the prison and had a fearsome reputation, the man heaved himself out of his chair and left the room.

"Now, it's Steve, isn't it?" the visitor asked.

"Yes... Who the fuck are you?"

"Never mind that, for the moment. Tell me, Steve, would you like to get out of here?"

"You bet. Who wouldn't?"

"What would you be prepared to do to get out?"

"How do you mean?"

"Well, would you be prepared to join the Army, and fight in one of those wars we have all the time now?"

"Well, I guess so – anything would be better than being locked up in here."

"Would you be prepared to kill a man to get out?"

"Hey... That's different. It depends, I guess. If he was attacking me... But then, that's how I got put in here in the first place..."

"No, he wouldn't be attacking you. But if he were evil, and a real enemy of the USA?"

"Why should I care about the USA? It's the Government that's put me in here."

"Well, Steve, I guess you've got a point. But the Government will certainly keep you here, too, for the rest of your life. You do know that, don't you? They have to make 'life' mean 'life', if the new law and order policies are to mean anything. So do you really want to die in here? You're only 28, aren't you? And with a good diet, lots of exercise, and absolutely no stress, you'll probably live until you're 80! Over 50 more years, Steve. How does that feel?"

I was speechless. I guess it probably hadn't occurred to me like that before – and he was right. The diet here, although plain, was actually good for you. I did exercise. And there was absolutely no stress for me – all I did was get up, work out, eat, and sleep. I probably would live a long life.

"I've got a deal for you, Steve. In return for your co-operation – your ACTIVE co-operation – in a plan we're constructing to help the USA with an Arab nation, we'll have the Supreme Court look at your case again, and decide to hear it. When they do, they'll decide the evidence of the shooting was ambiguous, and order you to be released."

"Look, who the fuck are you? Where in the Government do you come from?"

"Never mind that. All you have to know is that I'm part of a special operations group that has the power to make things like that happen. Now, are you interested, or am I wasting my time?"

"Of course I'm interested. But exactly what are you going to make me do? I'm not a murderer – I won't kill a guy in cold blood, even if you tell me he's a enemy of the government."

"We won't ask you to do that. That's my job, if it needs to be done. Now, time is short. Are you interested, or shall I leave here, and leave you to live out the rest of your life?"

"Well, I'd have to take a deal like that, wouldn't I?"

He stretched out his hand, saying "Well, shake on it then, partner".

I reached out mine and felt his handshake, which was firm and determined. Underneath the expensive suit I could see that he was actually a pretty fit looking guy, and his handshake hinted at hidden power and strength. He was shorter than me, only about 6'0," and his body was generally smaller than mine, but, nevertheless, he was still a pretty good specimen I guessed.

"I'm David, by the way," he went on, "But my friends all call me Dave. Now, I assume you've got nothing here you want? No special possessions or anything?"

I hadn't had much before I was locked up, and I hadn't been allowed to bring anything with me anyway to the prison.

"No..."

"Right then, we're out of here."

Dave went to the door, opened it, and told the governor he could come back in to his office.

"I'm leaving now, with the prisoner, as we discussed," to simply said.

I was expecting the governor to say something, or go on about procedures, or delay in some way, but he just gave a little shrug.

"On your head be it," he commented. "You brought the right papers, and I can't stop you. Although, if you ask me, I think it will end in disaster."

"Well, governor, fortunately no-one is asking you. Now, tell your guards to let us out."

We were out of the prison within minutes, and waiting in the visitors' car park outside the gate was a pretty neat looking late-model sports car.

"Get in," Dave told me, and I slid into the luxurious leather of the contoured passenger seat.

He started the engine to get the air conditioning going, then reached over to the glove box and took out a metal bracelet.

"Give me your arm over here"

"What for?"

"Look, Steve, you've got to learn. I give the orders. When I tell you to do something, you do it. It's easy enough to have you re-arrested as an escaped convict, and you'd be back in there within hours. Now, give my your arm."

"Hey, man, no-one would believe I could escape from that place... There'd be a lot of questions asked about how I got out... That governor would tell... So I do have some say in what goes on you know... I..."

"Shut it, Steve! And listen, and listen well. If you are too much trouble, we will arrange for you to be re-arrested. But, sadly, as the officers close in, you'll get violent and they'll reluctantly have to use their weapons. Dead bodies don't ask awkward questions, and I doubt it will even be a paragraph in the local paper. You've seen how I can get you out of prison – do you think an organisation like mine, that can simply ignore the law like that, would hesitate to have you killed?"

I knew he was right, and I pushed my left arm towards him. He put the metal band around my wrist, and there was a "snick" as it snapped shut. I pulled my arm away, and looked – there was now a smooth band of stainless steel about an inch wide, and relatively thick, around my wrist – it felt thick and heavy as it hung there, and I was very conscious of it. There were no obvious fastenings, and no visible means of getting it off again. Engraved on it, in small, precise letters, were the words "Property Of The Government Of The USA".

"Sorry about that, Steve, but it's regulations. There are some that are worried about having a dangerous criminal, a double murderer as they think of you, roaming around. So that's a special tracer bracelet that continuously broadcasts your position to the GPS satellite system. You can't get it off, as you will see – it was made to your measurements, and has an internal lock – once it's on, it can only be got off by cutting it off, and I don't think you'll easily find a saw for that metal – it's specially hardened."

"You assumed a lot... Having that bracelet made... I mean, how did you know I was going to accept?"

"Look, Steve, you may be pretty dumb to go on leading a kind of wild life with all the new laws, and you may not have gone to college, but you're not stupid! Anyone with even a glimmer of intelligence offered at least a chance of getting out of that place was bound to accept, and so I came prepared. Whether you stick it out is another matter!"

"What do you mean?"

"Well, you've already told me you won't kill to stay out. But we've yet to find out what else you won't do. Maybe there are too many things you won't do, and we'll have to give up on you, dispose of you, and start off with another convict. It would be a pity, as you have certain advantages... But not impossible. So remember, every time you're told to do something, is the price of not doing it worth the risk?"

"What advantages? What are you going to ask me to do?"

Dave sort of looked at me, but shifted the car into gear and we roared off down the highway – I was pushed back into the seat by the power of the acceleration.

We drove on for about an hour and were soon on the Interstate, heading East.

"We've got a 12 hour journey," Dave remarked. "We're heading for the training base for our mission, down in Arkansas. We ought to fly, really, rather than being stuck in this car. But we've got paranoid about leaving any trace of movements around – so no flights that could be traced on commercial airlines, no specially requested army helicopter movements, nothing. Just the two of us, on this boring Interstate."

"Hey, it's fine by me. It may boring for you, but after that prison..."

"Have you travelled much before?"

"No, I mostly stayed around my home town. There wasn't a lot of money for travel. Anyway, why Arkansas? What base?"

"Steve, no questions. But I'll tell you it's Arkansas as it's easy to run a covert base down there out in the wild hills. Folks don't ask too many questions. Now, are you comfortable? Too hot, too cold?"

"No, I'm fine. Won't you tell me more about this?"

"NO. You'll find out more, once we get to the base. But don't worry – we'll train you properly, and, think about it, whatever there is is better than spending the rest of your life in that prison, isn't it."

"Training?" I got no reply. Dave just half turned towards me, and grinned.

"Yes, I'm particularly looking forward to training you. And, provided you relax, you'll enjoy it too."

He didn't seem inclined to say more, though, and we barrelled along the Interstate. I guess to anyone looking in to the car we probably looked like a couple of studs on the way to a hot date, and no one would think we were some sort of Government spook and a convicted murderer!

Part 2

We'd been driving for about two hours, when Dave pulled in to a rest area and we got out, stretching our legs. He bought me coffee and a burger – man, was it good! It was the first "proper" food I'd had for months, and I tore into it, letting the juice dribble down my chin.

Dave watched me closely as I ate. "I'd buy you another one, Steve, but we don't want to get you into bad habits. We want you lean and fit, just as you are now after the prison regime. All that fat isn't good for you, you know."

"Sure, I know. But when you haven't had a burger for months..."

Dave grinned at me again, and we went to the rest rooms. Even though the place was almost empty, he stood at the next urinal to me – it was almost as if he wanted to look at my dick! I couldn't help sneaking a peak at him, either, as you do – not that I'm interested in men's dicks, it's just one of those things that all guys do, isn't it? You want to know how you compare with the others. Dave was cut, unlike me, and had nothing to be ashamed of – his dick seemed to go well with the rest of his well-proportioned body. He zipped up, but I stood there a few moments longer, still massaging the last drops of piss out from under my foreskin.

We went out to the car, and there was a gang of bikers standing near it, looking at it closely.

"Hey, look at that – a couple of fags, in a real fag car," one of them said as we approached.

Dave just ignored them, but I felt my anger starting to rise.

"Do you two recline those fancy seats before you suck your dicks?" the biker went on, and his buddies all started to laugh. Dave ignored them, and opened the door. The chief biker stepped forward and put his hand on Dave's shoulder. "Hey, fag, I asked you a question. Do you recline..."

He never got to the end of the sentence, because Dave whirled around and, before I could see what happened, he somehow hit the biker so he just collapsed onto the ground. Three others made to set on Dave, but they too all ended on the floor, in a heap.

"Get in, Steve," Dave said, and he was not even breathing hard. "No... Get in the driver's seat. You would like to drive, wouldn't you? I'd like to massage my knuckles a bit after those stupid fuckers tried to upset my day."

"How did you do that...," I started to ask. "Will they be OK? Should we call the cops...?"

"Just drive, Steve."

I started the engine, and pulled away. Man, it was amazing – the feeling of power from that incredible machine. I'd never driven a car like this before.

"To answer your question, Steve," Dave said as we screamed out of the on-ramp on to the Interstate, "It's just training. Those guys thought they were tough, but I've been trained in unarmed combat. And I'm pretty fit, too, you know."

The car felt fantastic under my control, and every time I hit the accelerator the surge of power pushed me back into the seat. The steering was light and precise, and sitting low down, being very close to the road, it was almost like driving a go-cart. I pushed the car harder and harder, and once I had shifted into 6th gear, was flashing along at 120 mph – and even then, the machine was ready to accelerate.

Dave said nothing, just sat there, kneading his knuckles, with a look of quiet satisfaction on his face. As we went past the next on-ramp there was a highway patrol car, and he started his light and siren as we went past.

"Don't worry, Steve, he can't catch you," Dave grinned. And I could see he was right – the patrol car was falling further and further back. But about 10 miles ahead they'd set a road block – the Interstate was straight for miles there on the plains, and lightly loaded, and so I could see them clearly.

"Better stop, Steve," Dave said. "All they can do is lock you up, after all!"

But they didn't – there was a lot of shouting as we pulled up, and the officers spread us both against the side of the car and frisked us roughly. There was a lot more shouting when a large automatic was found under Dave's jacket. They went to cuff us, but Dave said, very authoritatively, "Before you make complete asses of yourself, look in my wallet".

I thought the patrolman was going to hit him, but I guess there must have been something in Dave's tone. The man opened Dave's wallet, and saw some kind of government badge inside.

"Now, get on your radio, officer, and ask your dispatcher to look up the meaning of that code that's printed on my card. And do it before you do anything else to me and my companion, and before you get yourself into any more trouble."

Well, it took a few minutes, but the patrolman ultimately came back to us from his car and said "Sorry, SIR. I've been told to ask you if you need any further assistance from the patrol, SIR."

"No, officer. We'll be on our way."

We drove off, and Dave made a point of accelerating up to a high speed as the patrol officers watched us leave.

"Hey – how did you do that?

"Steve, that's another lesson for you. The agency I work for has complete immunity to the normal laws. Even in everyday things like speeding tickets! Remember that, if you feel like doing anything stupid in the next few weeks – we have total authority to do whatever is necessary to complete our work."

We drove on in silence for a couple more hours, then Dave pulled off the Interstate and we headed into a medium-sized town.

"We can't make it back to back tonight, so we'll find a motel," Dave told me.

———————————

It was a pretty standard room, I guess – two double beds, bathroom, TV. But this was an expensive motel – there was a pool, and a gym. Dave had a small bag with him, but I had no luggage, of course.

"Want to swim, or use the gym?" Dave asked.

"Yes, but I've got no gear..."

He opened his bag, rummaged around, pulled out a pair of black Speedos, and tossed them to me.

I held them up and looked at them – I'd worn Speedos when I was in the swimming team at High School, but these looked small even compared to the ones I'd worn then – and I'm a lot bigger and more muscular now than I was in those days.

"Well, I don't know... These don't look the right size..."

"Oh don't be stupid – they'll stretch. And they're only a token to pander to the natives' prudery, just so you can say you've got something on. I don't suppose there will be any people watching us anyway."

As he was saying this, Dave had produced another pair from his bag, had taken off his jacket, and was unbuttoning his shirt. He slipped it off, and I could see that I had been right about his physique – there wasn't an ounce of fat on him, and his belly was taught and firm. He slipped off his shoes, unbuckled his belt, and stepped out of his pants to stand there in his socks and cotton boxers.

"Come on, Steve... Not coming for a swim?"

Completely unconcerned, he pushed his thumbs behind the waistband of his boxers and pushed them down over his hips to let them drop to the floor. He stepped out of them, and bent over and pulled each sock off, to stand there naked. I couldn't help seeing how muscular his thighs were as he stooped to reach his feet, and how unconcerned he was at displaying his body like this.

"Hurry up, Steve..."

I started to unbutton my shirt. It felt strange – obviously I've changed all my life in the changing room at school, and at the gym, and of course in prison. So I'm used to having guys see me naked, and seeing others strip, too. But somehow it's different in a motel room – the two beds there, with Dave's clothes strewn around made it seem somehow more... more... intimate, I think might be a good word.

Dave was unselfconsciously fiddling with his tackle – teasing his dick away from his balls, and giving a little stroke of his balls to free them, then pulled on his Speedos. He stood there, his long limbs and muscular body perfectly complemented by the shiny black polyester of the slip, and watched me.

It's reflex, isn't it? Whenever you have your dick out you always just tug at it, and even though Dave was next to me, I did it. He seemed to be watching me, and I felt faintly embarrassed.

The Speedos gripped me as if they were made of rubber, because they were too small for me really. They were only just right for Dave, and on my bigger frame they were almost obscene. My dick was clearly outlined through the straining fabric, and the top of my pubic bush was almost visible above the low-cut front.

Dave saw me looking concerned, and said "Hey, man, don't worry – you look great! And anyway, in those motel pools there are never many people: it's just a few studs like us who want to exercise before dinner". He started towards the door of the room, and then, seeing me hesitating, came back and sort of ushered me along, with his arm around my shoulders in a "buddy" kind of way. Looking back after what I now know, I can see I was being very stupid, and Dave must have been roaring with laughter inside at my shyness about my body.

We went out to the pool, and it was great – I hadn't swum for a couple of years, and having the water around me felt fantastic. Dave was a very competent swimmer, and we started to race each other, lap after lap, up and down the pool. Neither of us wanted to be the first to give up, and we were two athletic guys trying to show each other who was the fastest, and the fittest, and indulging in that manly competition that two guys always end up doing.

I could have gone on for much longer, but Dave actually had better technique and was a whole length ahead of me when he stopped and stood there in the shallow water. I finished my length, and went and stood beside him, and we both grinned.

"Feeling better after being shut up in that prison, and that drive today?" Dave asked.

"Man, that was fantastic. I'd forgotten what it's like to be in the water. They don't provide pools in the US Prison Service!"

"Fancy a Jacuzzi, then?"

"Sure."

Dave pressed his palms on the pool edge, and effortlessly leaped out of the water, and I followed. The Jacuzzi was actually in the changing room, not the main pool area, and we went in and Dave turned on the pump. I went to get in, but he shouted at me

"You've got nothing to be ashamed of, you know – get those Speedos off! Real men don't wear them in a Jacuzzi!"

As he was speaking, Dave had pushed his Speedos down and was making his way into the bubbling water, totally naked. Shrugging my shoulders, I did the same – it seemed funny, actually, because on the few occasions when I'd been with a High School team to a hotel we'd always worn our shorts in the Jacuzzi.

We stood there in the hot water, side by side, and as guys do, we spread our arms along the edge of the tub and let our feet float free. I can't remember what we were chatting about – nothing important, anyway, but to make ourselves heard above the noise of the rushing water, we moved closer together perfectly naturally, and soon our outstretched arms were lying together along the pool edge.

As Dave's toes bobbed above the water, I could also see his dick breaking the surface, and I let mine do the same, too. We both half lay there, looking at each other.

"So your parents didn't have you cut when you were a kid," Dave observed.

"No – I don't think they could afford the doctor's fees. All the other guys at school used almost to laugh at me – until we were older, and started jerking off. Then when I told them how it was so easy, with all that natural lube... They got quite envious!"

Dave's other hand reached down and felt his dick, and he kind of fondled the head between his thumb and forefinger. He looked as if he was starting to get an erection.

"You're a lucky man, Steve. Guys often tell me that its better with a foreskin. I'll never know, as I was cut as a baby, so I've only got the 'after' and no 'before' to compare it with."

I reached down, too, and started fiddling with my own dick – I don't know why. I'd never joined in any of the circle jerks at school or anything like that, and I certainly wasn't going to jerk myself off in a Jacuzzi, even if Dave did. But when you see one guy playing with his dick, somehow it seems natural to do the same with yours, doesn't it?

We looked at each other, and it was Dave who made the decision. "Come on, Steve – I don't think the motel would be very pleased if they had the water in their Jacuzzi mixed with cum. We'd better get out!"

As he spoke he climbed out of the water up the steps, and I could see all the muscles in his strong legs and firm ass moving as he did so. He seemed to be completely unselfconscious, and stood there on the edge of the pool, still stroking himself slowly. I got out, too, and I could see him watching me closely as I did.

"You sure have a good body, Steve. I can see why you were selected," he told me.

"Selected for what?"

He hesitated for a moment: "Why, for this mission... Anyway, let's towel off, and get dinner."

He didn't bother to put his Speedos back, and strode off towards our room with just one of the small towels draped around his waist – his tackle made a big bulge at the front, and as he walked the sides of the towel moved to show his powerful thigh. I would have put my Speedos back on – actually, I wouldn't have taken it off in the first place – but I did the same. It's funny, isn't it, how different it feels when your dick and balls are swinging free, without underwear or pants to confine them?

Back in our room Dave was towelling himself dry finally, and as he dried his short hair I could see his dick waving around in response to the movements of his body – he still seemed totally unconcerned about having me there with him in this very intimate space, and that made me feel relaxed, so I pulled the towel away from my waist and did the same.

I don't think there has ever been a better steak than that one he bought me that night, and with a few beers inside me as well I felt on top of the world. I'd never known before how much being "free" meant, and now I was seeing more of life, too, the life too where men bought motel rooms and good dinners without worrying about the money, where they drove exotic sports cars, and where they had the power to do what they wanted, when they wanted. It was a heady mixture, and I was so envious of Dave.

"Tell me about yourself," I said after my fifth beer. "You know as much about me, I guess, as I know about myself. What about you? How did you get his mysterious job you have? And is there a 'Mrs. Dave' waiting for you at home?"

"No, that would be telling," he said grinning at me in a friendly way. I noticed that he'd had only a single beer all evening, and was not as relaxed as I was.

"Aw, come on. I won't tell on you!"

"Well, I'm pretty conventional, I guess. High School, a good college. I was going to go into the Air Force as a career, as I wanted to see the world a bit. But after my initial tests, I was asked if I wanted to join this special department. The selection tests were really tough – not exams or anything, but a few weeks seeing if I could survive in all kind of different places – jungles, deserts, and so on. I don't really like talking about it – probably because I don't really like remembering it. That's where I've been ever since. I was chosen for the job – I didn't pick it."

"So what about 'Mrs. Dave'? What does she think about it?"

"There is no 'Mrs. Dave', Steve. I never had time to meet anyone – too busy working to get top grades at school and college, I guess. And the job since then – well, it's not really conducive to long term relationships."

"Anyway," he went on, "Time to turn in. We've got a long day tomorrow."

I was disappointed, as I'd hoped we go to the bar and, if I could persuade him to have another drink, I might have found out more about what this special assignment was all about. As it was, though, we went straight back to our room and got ready for bed – Dave didn't seem to be at all concerned about stripping totally and getting into one of the beds completely naked – I guessed he was like a lot of guys, who've given up wearing anything at all in bed. I was used by now to sharing a small cell with others, so being in a large room with Dave was fine. As I started to jerk myself off as I always did before going to sleep, I felt certain I could hear those unmistakable rustles from the other bed that told me Dave was doing the same thing.

I slept well, in the big luxurious bed, and just didn't wake up properly – I was in that half-awake, half-asleep doze when I heard Dave showering, and several requests from him to "Get out of the sack," "The shower's free," and so on. But I just lay there, only half awake. The next moment, though, I was wide awake – Dave had pulled the covers of me to expose my naked body, and had slapped my bare ass quite hard, shouting "Come ON, Steve, we've got to be on our way" as he did so. I was lying on my stomach, and the slap was quite hard and caused me to give a little yelp of surprise. But the worse thing was then having to turn over and get off the bed – I had my usual morning hard-on, and I could see Dave looking at my swollen dick as it reached for the sky.

"Hey, don't worry, Steve – I've seen a guy's dick before, you know," he said as he saw my embarrassment. "Now, get your lazy ass into the shower – we've got to hit the road!"

He let me drive again that morning, and knowing that he had the magic "Get out of jail free" card, I didn't spare the engine on the car, and we flashed along the Interstate in almost no time.

When we finally turned off onto the Arkansas state highways Dave took over, and without looking at a map navigated us along successively smaller and smaller roads – I wondered where this base of his was going to be, as we went through tiny hick towns and then finally up a steep road into the low hills surrounding the valley we were in. All of a sudden there were two armed guards at a gate – and they looked like proper guards, marines, who obviously meant business, not those tired old private security men.

Dave showed his pass again, and the guards waved us through, throwing him a crisp salute as they did. We drove on for what seemed like quite a way, and there were buildings hidden in the trees and signs of a lot more of the tough-looking marines exercising, jogging between the buildings, and generally observing what was going on. We stopped in front of a large, totally featureless building – one storey tall, but with absolutely no visible openings in the outside of it except for the door, through which we entered.

There were more of the tough-looking marines inside, and Dave's pass was again inspected. He tossed the car key onto the desk they were at and told them he wouldn't be needing the car again for several weeks, as "he was back in the routine". The guards laughed at this, as they obviously knew what he meant, and Dave led me on down a series of hallways that were empty except for closed doors at intervals to the left and right.

I guessed we must be in the heart of the building when we stopped in front of one of these doors, and Dave put his palm against a panel to its right. There was a click and the door opened, and we went in. I was amazed – it was just like a motel room again, only slightly larger as the only bed had a lot of space around it. But there was a desk, a TV, and a row of curtains along one wall where the windows would be. I moved over and pulled them aside – but they covered a blank wall.

Dave laughed as he saw this, and told me "We use this guest suite for all kinds of purposes, so we make it as much like a motel as possible. This will be our home for the next few weeks, whilst we get you ready."

"Get me ready? What the hell's going on? Am I going to be stuck in this room for the next few weeks, do you mean? And you said 'we' – are you going to be here, too? " As I said this, I was looking around and, plainly, there was only the one double bed.

"So many questions, Steve. And I guess now is as good a time as any to tell you what this is really all about. Why don't you sit down, as I think it's going to be a bit of a shock to you!"

I went and slumped in the big armchair, and he went on "Do you know what big fancy politicians and international leaders do when they meet?"

"You mean like for international summits and so on...? I guess they sit down and talk to each other."

"Yes, Steve, that's the real purpose. But international protocol means there's a lot of other things, too – when the President's plane touches down in another country he reviews an honour guard on the tarmac. There's a ceremonial drive into the city. A big state banquet. And the talks, of course. And do you know what else?"

"No."

"Well, the leaders exchange gifts. Most presidential palaces, government offices, and even the White House, are stuffed with these things that leaders exchange. And there's even a special office in the State Department that liaises with the other country before the President goes, on the type of gift that would be suitable. For some countries, like Britain, it's just a plaque or something, and their Prime Minister gives us a piece of glassware, or a Wedgwood plate, or something like that. But in the less civilised world, the gifts can be large, and expensive – potentates and dictators expect to get something they can use personally, like a diamond-encrusted Cartier watch. The US Governemnt spends a lot on these gifts, and they're important in smoothing the progress of the talks – they're expected, and part of international protocol."

"Yes, so..."

"Well, during a recent visit to the USA, the son of one of the Arab rulers was with a party looking at our prison system. He visited the prison you were in, and he saw you working out. He tried to buy you, there and then, but of course he couldn't!"

"Buy me?"

"Yes, slavery is still legal in their country. They don't have prisons as such – rather, guys like you who are sentenced to life imprisonment are sent instead as indentured labourers to work down the mines and so on. So it was natural to think that you, being a life prisoner, would be available for such a contract."

"You're kidding, right – this is some sort of joke...?"

"No, Steve, it's more serious than that. When he got home, he told his father about how we had slighted the honour of his family by refusing to do business with him. His father was really pissed off, as he idolises his only son. And he got his Minister For External Affairs to complain to the US Government! Of course, nothing could be done, and the row was dying down. But then everything changed."

"Changed...?"

"Yes. We need the support of that country to help us negotiate the general Middle East peace process, and the ruler said that if he was to do that, the President would have to ask him himself. So the President is going on a State Visit in six weeks... And when the State Department started to ask about a suitable gift to exchange, they were told that the only acceptable one was you! The ruler had engineered the meeting to get the one thing his son wanted that he couldn't buy for him!

"You really are joking, right? Surely the President would just say that you can't give a guy away..."

"No, Steve. The deal is too important. And we can't back out now, as there would be too many questions asked about why a meeting like this was cancelled by the USA. So I'm afraid that you're going to be spending the rest of your life in hotter climates!"

"No. I won't. Take me back to prison."

"That's not an option, Steve, as I just explained. Try to think of it positively – you were destined to spend the whole of the rest of your life locked up in that prison. This way, at least, you get to see a bit of the rest of the world, and you'll meet new people, do different things..."

"You said 'work down the mines'. Doesn't sound much different from prison to me!"

" No, Steve, I said that criminals in their country usually ended up down the mines, or something. The ruler's son has a different plan for you, obviously. Why do you think he wants you?"

"I've no idea."

"Well, we've looked at the surveillance tapes of the visit, and we saw the way he looked at your body. And our intelligence service tells us that although he has five wives and several children, to secure the succession, he actually only fucks them when he needs to breed. He takes his sexual pleasure with men... And so it's certain that he won't send you to the mines – your body is too special for that. You'll become his sex toy."

"Fuck NO! I'm not going with guys. I've never had sex with men. I'm straight, not some fucking faggot..."

"That's why you're here, Steve. We're going to teach you to behave properly, as a 'toy', in the next few weeks. That, and modify you slightly to make you into a more suitable gift..."

"Fuck no, I'm out of here!"

I leaped out of the chair and went to the door – but there was no handle on the inside!

Part 3

I slammed my fists into the door in desperation, and shouted for someone to come and let me out. Dave simply watched for a few moments, then said "OK, Steve, let's cut all this crap, shall we? You saw where we are when you came in – you're right in the middle of a tightly-guarded government building in the middle of a secret base. We do lots of thing here that would not necessarily be approved of if it was written up in The Washington Post, or if it came on the TV screens. We're used to doing all sorts of things – normally to prisoners and agents we've captured, but sometimes to guys like you, too. You're not the first guy to be shipped off as a sex toy, you know! We have to keep Arab governments sweet, and if they see any guys they fancy, like when they're visiting the UN in NYC, we'll do what we can to supply them."

"And what have you got to lose?" he went on. "Sure, you're relatively happy in that prison now because you haven't been here that long and are still managing to keep yourself occupied working on that body of yours, and watching TV. But do you want to do that for he rest of your life? Will you still be working out when you're 70, or will you just sit slumped in front of the TV all day? And by then, with no outside contact, you won't even know what half the things are for – imagine what it must be like for cons now who see everyone using cell phones, when those came along after they were locked up! Well, with the pace of change in our country, there are going to be even more things like that in your future."

"But I'm not some sort of slave, to be given away..."

"Yes you are, Steve. Your whole life belongs to the Government. You have been sentenced to life imprisonment, and that's exactly what it is, remember: there's no parole, no possible reduction in sentence. The Government houses you and feeds you, and basically forgets you. You no longer have any money, any rights... Nothing. You are effectively controlled and owned by the Government, and if it chooses to give you away..."

"No, I say. I'm a free man..."

"You were a free man, Steve, before you were sentenced. Now you're nothing. And I'm tired of this debate. Get out of those clothes, so we can start."

"What do you mean?"

"Look, I've told you before that I know you're not stupid. Don't make me revise my views. When I say 'get out of those clothes', I mean just that: strip. Get naked. I want to inspect you, and see how much work has to be done on you, to prepare you."

"Fuck you! I'm not a slave, I tell you. I'm not getting naked in front of you..."

"You're wrong, you know. You've already started down the route to slavery. You did it when we left the prison: look at your wrist – you have a standard slave locator band, as they use throughout Arabia, on there now. And I know you're not body-shy – I saw you naked lots yesterday, and, and a very nice sight it is too! So get out of those clothes."

I glared at him, went and slumped in the armchair again, and folded my arms.

"I'm really sorry about his, Steve... ". Dave looked up into the corner of the room ,where I could then make out a miniature TV camera poking through the ceiling tiles. "Guards... Get in here."

The door opened, almost instantly, and four of the tough-looking marines came in. They never said anything, just came over towards me – then they grabbed me! Now, as I've told you, I'm no stranger to a bit of bar-room brawling, but against these four trained guys I didn't have a chance. Within seconds I had been dragged out of the chair, rolled on the floor, and stripped – they weren't violent, or anything – they just seemed to naturally prevent me from landing a punch, they avoided my flailing legs, and quickly and efficiently stripped all the clothes off me. Then they looked at Dave, who nodded in assent, and they left.

Dave was standing above me as I lay there on the floor. "Let that be a lesson to you. We can do all of this the hard way, or you can co-operate and make things easier for yourself. Every room we'll be in is constantly monitored, and I only have to call for the guards, and they'll be in on the job in seconds."

I started to get up, and stood there in front of him. "Look, Dave..."

"Silence! Let's start this training the way it's going to go on. From now on, you only speak when you're spoken to. You are respectful to me at all times. And you refer to me as 'Boss'."

I was so amazed by this, I just sort of shut up, and he went on "Firstly, then, I want to see you cum. I heard you jerking off last night, and I saw that dick of yours erect this morning. But I want to see it all together. Jerk off for me."

"Fuck you..."

"We'll get on to fucking later. But I'm disappointed to see you've forgotten my rules already... That wasn't very respectful, was it? Now, are you going to jerk yourself off, or am I going to get those marines back in here? They do quite a good job, you know – three of them hold you down, whilst the other one jerks you off. That can be quite rough – you'll soon find out that no one really is as good at jerking you off as you are yourself, and those big, horny hands they have can be quite painful. Still, I know they'll enjoy it – we choose the marines who come here on a rather special basis, you know – none of them is married, for example... And I'm sure they're itching to get heir hands on you, after they've seen you lying there naked. Now – are you going to jerk yourself off...?"

I knew he meant what he said. What was I to do? I could see that there was no way that I could fight my way out of here, or even stand up to those marines. I turned around, so my back was to Dave, and reached down for my dick.

"No, slave! Another lesson for you. A slave never turns his back on his master! I want to see that dick of yours – turn around. You need never be embarrassed or ashamed by anything to do with your body in front of your master."

I turned, slowly, and I felt a rush of blood to my head. I knew that my shoulders, neck and face were starting to glow red with embarrassment. I just stood there, gently stroking my dick, and to my surprise, I felt it starting to go hard – actually, I suppose it is quite erotic to be so under the control of another guy that you must do exactly as he tells you, even though it is one of the most intimate things you do with yourself.

"That's good, Steve. You'll soon learn to lose any inhibitions you have about your body. And that will make the later stages of your training easier, when I teach you all about sex."

"I already know all about sex..."

"Slave, shut up! If you interrupt me again, or fail to refer to me as boss, I'll have those marines in here and have you spanked. And you're wrong anyway – you know nothing about sex. All you know about is fucking women – we know, from having watched you in prison, that you've never had real sex, proper man-to-man sex, that is. I'm looking forward to teaching you that!"

I went to say something – but I was too stunned. What did he mean – "proper" sex, man-to-man? I'm not some sort of faggot, after all. But Dave was going on "You may as well learn the right way to jerk yourself off, when a master tells you to, now we've got over that little emotional outburst. Unless he tells you otherwise, you assume the supplicant position... Now, kneel down, put your heels together, and spread your knees apart. Then rest backwards, so that your ass presses into your heels, and keep your body nicely upright."

I suppose I realised there was nothing else to do, so I got down onto the carpet and felt it pushing into my legs as I knelt, then shuffled to get my legs into the "V he'd talked about. It felt kind of strange to have my heels pressing into my but. I looked up at him, as he stared down at me.

"Good. Remember that position. Now, start to jerk yourself off. Use the hand you usually use, and use the other one to catch your cum as it spurts out – it's not that I'm concerned for the carpet, but most masters like their slaves to collect the cum."

So I did. I could feel myself getting redder and redder as Dave continued to watch me as I knelt there jerking my dick up and down. I thought I wouldn't get a complete erection, or, if I did, that I would never cum. But to my amazement my dick sprang into life as usual, and I felt myself starting to get to the point of climax.

"Stop a minute!" Dave commanded. He went over to the desk drawer and got something out, and came over to stand just behind me. "Right, off you go again, and be sure to catch that cum, remember – I don't want to have to have you spanked."

I started to jerk myself again, and suddenly Dave's hand was half over my face, and there was a strange, slightly antiseptic, slightly sweet smell. I went to twist away, but Dave snapped "Keep on jerking – don't mind what I'm doing."

The next moment I felt my flush of embarrassment getting hotter and hotter and my face going redder and redder. The most intense feeling of sexual excitement I'd ever known swept over me. I'd never felt like this before. It was if every sensation I'd ever known had been collected up and concentrated in my dick. A couple more strokes and I was shooting, uncontrollably. My heart was racing, and I felt fantastic. My body rocked backwards and forwards on my heels as I shot my cum into the palm of my hand. I couldn't stop myself – I moaned with animal excitement.

I realised I was breathing really hard – unusual, as I hadn't put all that much effort in to it – and that my heart was racing. In spite of everything, it was absolutely the best jerk-off I'd ever had. I'd forgotten Dave, I'd forgotten everything, as my whole body focussed down onto the pleasure sweeping through me, and that incredible sensation as you totally lose control as your balls jerk and pump your cum up and out.

"Good, Steve," Dave was saying. "A really good load. And you reacted well – you've never done poppers before, have you?"

I knew what poppers were, of course, as I'd read about them in the papers. But you couldn't buy things like that in our town, and I'd never got around to sending away for them by mail order.

"No, I've never done poppers...", and remembering what he'd said about spanking, I continued after a brief pause "...Boss."

"There, you see. There are things you don't know about sex. I bet that was the best jerk-off you've ever had, wasn't it? So, when I tell you about learning about proper sex, stop looking so worried. You'll enjoy that, too, as I'm a VERY experienced teacher!"

"You're going to have gay sex with me, Da... Boss?"

"You bet, Steve! It's part of my job. Normally I get the assignments where we want to 'turn' a diplomat or a spy, and we need to seduce him and take a few photos. All the guys and girls in my office think I'm really good at it, and they all have shots of me in action as the screen savers on their PCs! So, believe me, I'm fully experienced, and you'll enjoy it, when we get started."

"But for now, though...," he went on, "Just swallow that cum down, then get up."

"Swallow...?"

"Oh, come on, Steve.. Surely every guy has swallowed his own cum at some point, even if it as just when he was a kid and starting to jerk off, just to see what it's like."

"Well, I didn't, Boss... I can't... It's disgusting..."

"OK, this is your last chance! I'm really beginning to lose patience with you. Of course it's not disgusting. How can any fluid produced by your body be disgusting? But if you're not going to do it, we can have the marines in here and they'll feed it to you. And as some will inevitably get spilled as they do that, they'll have to add some of their own, so you have a really good load..."

Hesitatingly, trying to choke back the feeling of nausea I had as the smell of the stuff went up my nose, I raised my hand towards my mouth.

Well, as we all know, cum doesn't actually taste at all like it smells, and after my initial stomach-heaving reaction and when I had got control of myself, I ran my tongue over the pool in the palm of my hand and found it was just faintly salt, faintly sweet. After a moment's hesitation I simply licked away at it, and took it all down.

"See," Dave said. "That wasn't so bad, was it? Try and trust me, will you, and believe what I say? Real men always like cum, and you'll soon find out that taking cum from another guy, fresh and hot as it shoots out of his dick into your mouth, is one of the ways that brings an awful lot of pleasure to both of you."

I was appalled – I'd never thought that I would have to have another guy's dick in my mouth, and began to look worried.

"Anyway, that's for a later lesson," Dave said. "Let's go and eat."

He palmed a plate by the side of the door, and it opened and he stepped into the corridor. "Come on!" he snapped.

I stumbled around, trying to assemble at the clothes that had been torn from me, but they were ripped, and all the buttons had pulled away.

"Stop fucking around, Steve. You don't need those clothes. Slaves mostly go naked when they're sex toys, and the sooner you learn that the proper state for that body of yours is totally nude, on full display, the better. Now, follow me, to the marines' mess hall."

He stood there, looking at me, and I could see there was nothing else I could do. I didn't doubt he'd otherwise summon the marines and have me dragged there. So I moved out after him, and we strode off down the corridor – him in front, in his immaculate slacks and shirt, and me buck naked! I'd never felt more embarrassed as we went past sets of armed marine guards at key intersections, and they greeted Dave and just smiled at me – they didn't show any signs of thinking that having a naked guy there was at all unusual.

My dick swung up ands down as we were walking quite quickly, and it felt funny to have the carpet of the corridor against my naked feet. We went for quite a way, and I could start to hear a low noise of conversation in the distance. It got louder and louder, until Dave opened a door and I heard the full blast of it – there must have been about 30 guys in there, eating away at cafeteria tables.

Dave didn't stop, but motioned for me to follow him and join a short line of marines waiting to be served at a hatch in the wall. That was, I think, one of the hardest things I've ever done in my life – to walk across a room, stark naked, my dick bobbing up and down, with a room full of guys watching me. All eyes in the room turned to look at me, and it felt as if they were burning in to my naked body. But I obviously wasn't of great interest, as the marines soon returned to their meals and their talk amongst themselves.

Dave took a tray, but when I went to get one, he told me not to and just to stay in line and follow him. He went past all the dishes on display on the other side of the hatch, and chose salad, pasta, and fruit, and a bottle of beer. He only seemed to be selecting one of everything, and I went to tell him that I'd like one of the big steaks that were on display. Without any sign of anything being unusual he snapped at me "I told you, slave, never to speak to me unless answering a question. Any more of that and I'll get some of these guys to bend you over a table and spank you – they won't mind interrupting their break time for that!" He obviously didn't care that the marines heard him referring to me as "slave" – and so I knew that this must be some very special sort of base as Americans would normally react if they heard such a word used.

At the end of the line Dave took a big empty glass and filled it with water at the fountain, then told me to follow him. He sat at the end of a long table with a group of marines at the other end, and told me to sit opposite him. He unloaded the food in front of himself, and pushed the glass of water across the table towards me. Reaching into the pocket of his slacks, he brought out two hard-looking things rather like those bone-shaped treats you can buy to feed large dogs.

"This is slave chow, Steve. Better get used to it now, as that's mostly what sex toys get fed on. It's completely nutritious, and will keep you fit and healthy. No fat, no sugar, lots of protein for energy, and packed with all the vitamins and minerals you need for bright eyes and a healthy-looking skin!" He sounded just like those adverts you see on TV for pet food.

"Even better, you'll see that you have to bite them very hard, and that keeps your teeth and gums in good condition. Your new master will almost certainly feed you like this as it not only keeps you fit and healthy, but it's clean and quick, too. And, of course, there's no taste or smell associated with it – there's no point in letting a sex toy feed on normal food, as you might end up with a bad taste, like onions or garlic, in your mouth, and that can be unpleasant for your master."

"Now," he went on, "Eat up! That's all you're getting until tomorrow morning."

The marines at our table had of course heard all this, and were watching as I picked up one of the hard lumps, and bit into it. It was difficult – I had to almost gnaw at it, then crunch it up. There wasn't much taste – it was just slightly salty, and tasted vaguely of meat. I had to wash it down with water, and I could see why Dave had brought me such a large glass. The marines continued to observe me, and I heard one of them tell his buddies that it looked even worse than field rations!

"One of the other advantages of giving you slave chow all the time," Dave went on, "Is that if your master does choose to reward you with some normal food, it's a real treat for you and you will find it utterly delicious. After weeks of eating only slave chow, even the tiniest scrap of fruit, or perhaps a tiny piece of chocolate, or even steak, will have you salivating. And if we take away the pleasures of eating, it makes the other pleasures of the flesh all the more important to you!"

Dave finished eating, then told me to follow him and we re-traced our steps along the corridors to our room. As we stood up from the table all talk stopped momentarily as we crossed the mess hall, but as we left, I heard the conversation start up again, and there was even some laughter.

Back in the room Dave said it was bed time, and told me to go and relieve myself, and shower. I went into the bathroom and started to close the door, but Dave almost kicked it open as he saw this.

"You've got to remember, Steve, that slaves don't have any feeling of modesty. You never try to conceal yourself from your master. If he doesn't want to see you pissing and crapping ,he'll say so. Otherwise you just do it. Now, let me see you squat on that commode.

I was flushing red all over. I'd never crapped in front of another guy before. Never! Even when I was in the team at school, and in prison – there was always at least a bit of privacy for these functions. But Dave stood there watching me, and as I did need to go, there was not much I could do about it. With a great effort I did manage to drop a couple, and Dave still watched me as I wiped myself clean.

"We'll teach you how to crap using the more normal 'hole in the ground' that slaves use, in a later lesson," he said conversationally. "Now, get under the shower."

As I stood there soaping myself, Dave stripped himself and sat on the commode. "See, he shouted to me, "Nothing to be ashamed of. It's perfectly natural, and a master doesn't hesitate to do this in front of a slave."

I'd finished showering by then, and went to pick up a towel to dry myself.

"NO!" Dave snapped. "You wait to see if your master wants you in the shower with him. As it so happens, I don't – tonight – so you stand there quietly and wait."

He showered, then dried himself with one of the big bath towels, then handed the wet towel to me. "We don't waste resources unnecessarily," he said, "And so you use your master's towel to dry yourself."

Now I know that there's no harm in it – after all, Dave was clean before he used the towel, so there couldn't be any germs or anything. But I hated using other guy's things, and it required a huge effort to force myself to pull the damp cotton all over me.

Dave stood there, naked like me, watching me. "And your face, Steve," he said finally. "You didn't dry your face. There's nothing wrong with that towel, you know – it's only been on my body, and yours. Let me see you bury your face in it to dry yourself, and breathe in the traces of our bodies."

I still hesitated, as the thought of this made me feel sick. "Please, Boss..."

"OK. I've had enough of this. Don't you understand yet that you're here to OBEY?"

Dave caught me by the wrist, and pulled me back into the bedroom. He pushed me so that I was standing bent over the back of the big comfy armchair, took a magazine off the coffee table and rolled it loosely into a cylinder, and then hit my bare ass with it! I was so surprised, I cried out, and went to stand up and turn on him.

"Stay, slave!" Dave snapped. "Either you stand there and take six of these strokes from me, or I get the boys in and let them do it with their marine belts..."

All I could do was bend back over, and Dave hit me five more times with the magazine. Then he made me go and look at myself in the big mirror on the wall, and look at my ass which had turned a fiery red. It wasn't so much that it hurt – well it did, actually – but it was more the sheer humiliation of having another guy spank me in his way.

"If you're as clever as I think you are," Dave said as I stood there looking at my red ass, "You'll remember this. I don't like having to punish you, as I'd rather you submitted willingly to your lessons. But if I have to, I will. And you should remember that I can order much harsher beatings – and those marines actually look forward to it... Now, lie on the bed, not in it."

Dave joined me, and we lay side by side on the double bed, not quite touching. He picked up the TV Remote, and turned it on. "And another thing," he said, "You never use the TV yourself. Your master MAY allow you to watch TV with him, if he chooses, or, for example, I could make you stand in the corner of the room whilst I watch it alone. But I'm being nice to you tonight, and letting you lie here by me."

The TV was showing a hot porn film, and Dave explained that his was one specially made for "new recruits," like me. "It looks at first sight like normal, straight porn," he said. "But if you watch closely, you'll see that after the first guy has fucked her, he's joined by two other guys, and whilst they are playing with the chick, they're actually starting to get turned on by each other more. So it's something that both straight and gay guys can enjoy, and it starts to show you how men can bring pleasure to each other.

As we watched, both Dave and I got huge erections, and Dave started to jerk himself off.

"There's no more teaching tonight, Steve," he said conversationally. "I'm not going to start having you wank me, or suck me off, or anything. Just let's lie here like a couple of buddies 'back home' and each jerk ourselves off as we watch this. You used to do that, didn't you?"

"NO!"

"You mean you never had any buddies around for an evening's porn, and a bit of self stimulation and male talk?"

"NO! We wouldn't have exposed ourselves to each other..."

"Well, I thought all guys did that. Never mind, come on, enjoy the film. And make the most of this jerking off – it's the last time like that for you."

"Boss, 'last time'... What...?"

Dave didn't reply immediately as he was beating himself faster and faster in that way you do just before you shoot, then a big stream of his cum sprayed out. He'd pointed his dick along his body at the crucial moment, and his belly and chest were covered in his cum. I could smell that familiar aroma as it filled the room.

He stayed like that for a few moments, letting his breathing return to normal, then turned his head towards me. "Yeah. I forgot to tell you. I mentioned that we have to make a few changes to you – well, the primary one is that you have to lose that foreskin. It's not done in Arab countries to have a foreskin, and so yours has got to go. And you're scheduled for the snip tomorrow morning. So make the most of jerking yourself off with it on... You won't be able to do it again for about a week whilst the scars heal, and then it will all be different!"

With that, he clicked the TV off and rolled over on to his stomach – I guess he didn't worry whether the cum went all over the bed clothes or not. He buried his head in his arms, and said "So sleep well, and look forward to tomorrow!"

Part 4

The next morning Dave led me along the hushed corridors of the complex, nodding and acknowledging the greetings of the guards on the way – there seemed to be a lot of them around, and I wondered what went on behind all the other closed doors we passed that warranted such a concentration of manpower to make sure it remained secure.

I felt the soft carpet under my bare feet, and was very conscious of the air wafting past my naked body as we strode along. Interestingly, none of the marine guards seemed to find it at all unusual to see a totally nude guy in the corridors – it almost seemed to be an everyday occurrence as far as they were concerned. After several minutes we stopped and Dave pushed a button beside one of the doors, and a moment later there was the "snick" of an electric lock, and we were able to enter.

Inside there was a space that looked like a hospital emergency room – a couple of places for patients to lie, and lots of cabinets full of medical instruments and drugs.

"This is the patient, doc," Dave said cheerily to the man standing there – he was in green "scrubs," of the type surgeons use.

"Right, boy, up on this table," the guy who had answered to "doc" said to me, as he pointed at the leather-covered operating table in the centre of the room.

I hesitated, but Dave gestured to me to comply, making a little swishing movement with his hands to indicate that he'd think of spanking me again if I didn't do it. I knew it was useless to resist, as he held all the cards – even though I might have been able to overpower both him and the doctor, there was no way I could escape the regiments of marines who surrounded the place!

So I lay down, and felt the cool leather against my back and ass. The doctor took out a syringe and stabbed it into a small bottle, drawing a measured dose of some clear liquid into it. He then pushed on the syringe and allowed a few drops of fluid to squirt out of the end, as they always do in order to expel air from the needle.

"No, no anaesthetic!" Dave said. "An important part of his training is to learn that he is totally under the control of his master, and I want him to have an experience he will never forget. Whenever he doubts that he is a slave and starts to think of himself as a free man, I want him to snap back and remember what happened to him here – so no anaesthetic."

"I can't operate on a man without it," the doctor responded. "Even the marines, with iron self discipline, would jerk or move as soon as the scalpel touched them – and this boy has no incentive to stay still. It's too risky – one false move and his dick will be lying on the floor. No, let me give him just a tiny shot of a local anaesthetic to numb him."

"No, as I said, he's got to remember this. I don't want him to lose any part of the experience. We've learned that men like this don't truly accept that life has changed totally for them until they see that we have the power to even cut and mutilate their bodies if we wish to. So it's essential that he experiences everything, with no loss of sensation. But I accept what you say about his flinching and movement."

With this, Dave opened the door into the corridor and called for some of the marines standing out there to come in and join us. I heard him saying something to the four men who had appeared, and there was a lot of laughter from them. They came over and stood beside the table on which I was lying, and the next moment, with almost no effort, they were all over me.

I ended up with marines squatting on the table and gripping me so that I was totally immobilised: one was straddling each of my thighs, one was sitting on my belly, and the fourth was astride me with his knees pressed into my shoulders. I could see the bulge of his dick through his uniform as his crotch was almost directly in my face, and my nose caught that faint smell of stale urine that most guys have on their clothes around there.

"There, doc," I heard Dave say. "Now he can't move. Shall we experiment, and make sure?"

Dave moved to stand by the table, and I screamed as my balls were squeezed. My body tried to convulse, by reflex, but the weight of the four marines on me made it impossible to move.

"There, doc," Dave went on, "As you can see, he's totally immobile down there. So get on and do it."

The doctor then said, in that quiet but worrying way that doctors have when they're talking about patients "Are you after a complete cut, or just a trim of the surplus that hangs beyond the end, so that his piss slit is exposed but his flange is normally covered?"

"A full 'high and tight', I think it's called," Dave answered. "The dick head is to be fully exposed at all times – he's going to an Arab, and that's how they all are. Try to make sure that it's as neat as possible, though, and have as little scarring as possible – he's got a magnificent dick, and I think that's why his new master wants him. It would be a shame to spoil it by a botched circumcision – take your time, and cut slowly and carefully."

"Shall I leave the fretum, or shall I take it out at the same time? If he's going to be a sexual slave, taking it out can help him stay on the job longer as there's not so much sensation for him."

"I hear what you say, doc, but I think it's better to leave it in. He may as well get what pleasure he can from his work, I think!"

The doctor pulled on a face mask and surgical gloves, then draped a green surgical sheet around my exposed middle. "I don't want your uniforms to get spattered with blood," he was telling the marines, "So pull the loose bits of this sheet around you and cover yourself."

He had a scalpel in his hand, and came and stood by me. "Don't worry, boy. It only takes a minute or so – I have to cut a lot of guys here, as I deal with all the agents who are being sent to the Middle East – we have to circumcise them all, in case they're captured: an uncut dick would be a real give-away. There'll be a sharp pain as I make the first cut, then it will happen again as I trim the foreskin to the proper length. And then it will be all over, except for when I spray the finished work with antiseptic – and then it will hurt like hell again for a few moments."

"This will make it easier for you – open your mouth."

He had a small bar of something that was black in his hands, and he went on "This is tough rubber, and you can bite down on it as I cut. It will help you to bear the pain. Open wide, so I can slip it in"

I did as he said, and tasted the rubber as he positioned the bar in my open mouth. Then he didn't wait for me to say anything, but moved down the table.

The next moment it was just as he had said: there was an excruciating pain from my dick, and every muscle in my body tried to jerk and spasm to do something about it. But I couldn't move, as the four marines were clamped around me so tightly. I wanted to scream and shout, but the rubber bit really did help – I clamped my jaws together in a vain effort to try to stop the pain, and could feel my teeth sinking just a little into the rubber, that was almost unyielding.

It can't have gone on for more that a minute or two, I suppose, but when you are in enormous pain time ceases to have any real meaning. I felt as if I had been there for ever, as sharp slashes of sensation from my dick ran all through me. I could feel sweat breaking out all over, and little cool rivulets of it seemed to be running everywhere on my body.

Then it was over – or, rather, there were no more episodes of sharp, stabbing pain – just a persistent ache from my dick, that went on and on. I guess here are several types of on-going pain: the dull ache from a bruise when soft tissue has been hit; the sharp agony from a damaged tooth; the hot throb it you hit your finger with a hammer. This pain surging from my dick had all the characteristics of all these different kinds of hurt, all at once.

"Just a few minutes more now, boy," the doctor said. "I've completed the cutting and the antiseptic, and now all I've got to do is bandage you up."

"I guess it's all right to give him something for the pain now, is it?" he went on, looking at Dave.

"Oh sure, of course. We're not sadists here!" Dave replied. Then, looking at me, he continued "As I said, I want this to be an experience you will always remember. The first time a man has his body modified against his will is very special, very symbolic. You now know that someone else is in complete control of you, someone else makes the decisions about what happens to you. There may be other instances when your master has you modified in future, but this is the first, and the one you will remember most. The doctor will give you a local anaesthetic in your dick to stop it hurting now, but it was important for you to experience your circumcision fully."

"You're lucky, though, that we are civilised here. On my last trip to the Gulf a pleasure slave who was sucking his master off lost concentration for a moment and let his teeth rake down the shaft of his master's dick. The master gave a little yelp of surprise, and of course this was a tremendous loss of face for him, doing so in front of me, a foreigner! He had to order the immediate punishment of the slave, and this was carried out there and then to show me that the master was indeed in complete control – he had four teeth from the top jaw and four teeth from the bottom jaw of the slave pulled out there and then, entirely without any pain relief. He said that that would remind the slave to focus on his work at all times, and, of course, the 'modification' he had ordered to the slave meant that the accident could never happen again, anyway!"

"Still," he continued, "Let's hope that nothing like that ever happens to you! I thought the slave was somewhat disfigured by the loss of the teeth. He couldn't speak properly afterwards, and if he ever did smile, it looked hideous. I had him suck me off later that night, though, and having his gums rub against me was certainly an interesting sensation."

"OK, guys, and thanks," he said, gesturing to the marines, and they climbed off me, to leave me lying there on the operating table.

The pain from my dick was indeed subsiding, and I looked down and saw a neat white bandage all over my dick, with a little tube coming out of the end.

"Leave that bandage on for a couple of days," the doctor was telling Dave. "It will heal much more quickly if it's left totally undisturbed. I've pushed a catheter half way along his dick so he can pee without disturbing the dressing. Come back in three days, and I'll remove it all."

I climbed down from the table, and it all felt very strange- I was no longer in actual pain, but I could feel something completely different from my dick. Perhaps it was the additional weight of the bandages and the tube – after all, you aren't usually aware of your dick at all, are you, unless you get an erection or something and feel it thrusting against your underwear?

"I know you like to have the slaves in training totally naked," the doctor was telling Dave, "But for these first few days it's not very sensible to let his dick flop around and bang into his balls and his thighs all the time Especially if you're going to start the exercise regime, you should give him something to support him – a jockstrap, or briefs, or something."

"Sure thing, doc – have you got anything here?"

The doctor went over to one of the cupboards and returned with a white jockstrap.

"This is left over from a penectomy I had to perform on a slave a couple of months back – he had no need of it when he left!" the doctor said, and I could tell he wasn't joking.

Dave handed me the jockstrap, and I went to put it on. I hesitated for a moment, seeing a faint piss stain inside the cup, but knew it was no use arguing, so I pulled it on. For a moment I was back in High School – standing in the changing rooms with the other guys on the team, some already dressed, and some still in their jocks because they had not yet showered. I felt the comforting tug of the elastic straps under my ass, and that characteristic lump of cloth under my asshole.

"Are you OK, Steve?" Dave then asked me.

"Sure, boss. Any guy would be OK when he's just been cut..."

"Stop complaining! I allowed you pain killers now, didn't I? Anyway, let's get on. You first training session is due... Follow me."

With that, Dave shook hands with the doctor, opened the door, and strode out into the corridor.

We went along more corridors, all guarded by marines, and ultimately went through a door that took us into a vast gym. There were rows and rows of exercise machines, just as you'd see in any suburban gym – the only difference was that here many of them were occupied by guys who were already in fantastic shape: no flabby executives, no overweight housewives, just hard-muscled guys pounding away at their exercises.

Dave went over to a trainer who was standing watching – you could tell he was in charge from the way he held himself. He just knew he was in even better shape than any of those exercising, and he was obviously supremely confident in his own abilities.

"This is the new boy," Dave said to the trainer, "Answers to the name of Steve. We've got about four weeks to get him in shape – he's not bad now, as you can see... He's had an active job, and that's given him quite a good body. But we need that final buffing of his muscles. I'm planning on having him spend the afternoons out on the assault courses with the marines, and the mornings here in the gym. OK?"

"Sure. Provided he works hard, four weeks is fine. I can see he's in pretty good shape already, as you say. But what's he doing in the evenings? Why don't you send him here then, too?"

The trainer was smiling as he said this, and Dave clearly understood what was happening. "Let's just say he has other lessons to be learned in the evening...," he replied.

Then, turning to me, Dave said "Right, Steve, I'm leaving g you in the capable hands of the gym instructor here. Then this afternoon you are going around the assault course with the marine trainees. We need to polish and refine that body of yours, and we only have a short time. So you're going to be worked VERY hard – and I don't want to hear reports of you shirking. Any failure to fully comply with the orders of the trainers, and you'll be punished."

Well, I've been to the gym on occasions (although my manual labouring job meant that I really got enough exercise without it as a rule), but I've never experienced anything like what I was put through that morning. I ran and ran on the treadmills, and lifted weights until my muscles were almost giving way with the effort. The gym instructor seemed to ignore all the other guys to focus all his attention on me – I got a personal service, and there was absolutely no time to relax: one exercise followed another, absolutely without a break.

Sweat was poring off me, and I could feel the elastic waistband of the jockstrap getting soaked in it. Little rivulets were making their way across my pecs and down my stomach to soak the pouch, too, and it felt oddly clammy as I worked away.

At the meal break, the trainer did however relent and I was allowed to stop – I just sat against the wall, completely exhausted. The concrete walls of the gym and the smooth plastic of the floor felt delightfully cool against my naked body, and I just sat there, chest heaving, whilst my body desperately tried to return to normal. The trainer threw a couple of the biscuits I had eaten before at me, and gruffly told me that I'd better eat, as I'd need all my energy for the afternoon – the assault course was, he said gleefully, even more of a test than the machines here in the gym. He also told me to go into the showers and drink "There's no point in washing that sweat off you, as it will soon be back," he added cheerfully, "But you do need to take on a lot more fluid – it's hot out there on the assault course, and we don't want you collapsing. The objective is to get you in great shape, not to kill you."

It's funny, but the other guys in the showers almost completely ignored me. They had been wearing normal sing lets and shorts all morning whereas I was naked except for the jockstrap, and this hadn't seemed to cause any comment. Now I was in the showers with them they continued to behave just as if I wasn't there – they all obviously knew each other, but I, as a stranger, was almost "not there".

The assault course that I was taken to in the afternoon was in use by the marines at the base who were using it to do their regular training. Except for me, who only had a jockstrap on, they were all in their full uniforms and carried rifles and backpacks. To some extent, therefore, I had and easier time than them as I only had myself to get around the course. But, on the other hand, without the protection of the military fatigues I felt very vulnerable.

Initially the marines all laughed and sniggered as they saw me joining in wearing only a jockstrap, and I felt extremely conscious that I was very exposed to their gaze – as I threw myself over the obstacles I could tell that they were able to see my exposed ass.

On and on it went – as soon as we had gone around once, we had to do it all again. The sun beat down, and I'm sure I could feel the white skin of my exposed ass starting to burn – my upper body and thighs were quite brown already, as I often worked on the site just in shorts and my work boots, but of course there was that complete band of pure white around my middle which had never previously been exposed to the sun.

I'd never done this type of exercise before, whereas all the marines were pretty much used to it, and so it was actually quite hard – you had to throw yourself over walls, belly crawl under strands of barbed wire suspended a couple of feet above the ground, run through a trough of clinging mud, and traverse an area by pulling yourself hand over hand on a long rope. I could see it was all excellent exercise, and I knew it was using my body in a way that the regular exercises in the gym that morning just could never do.

At the end of the afternoon the marine instructor told his men to climb into the back of a truck, and he and I were then standing there alone. "I guess you'd better join the boys up there," he told me. "I can't leave you out here alone, and there are no other instructions as to what to do with you."

So I climbed aboard, and the marines were really nice guys – they chatted to me, and congratulated me on "surviving" the afternoon! Even so, they were somewhat cautious and it was almost as if they knew they should not ask why I was only wearing a jock, or, indeed, what I was doing joining in their training at all.

We crossed the base and drew up in front of a marine accommodation block, and the guys all leapt out. Having nothing better to do, I followed them and we all went into their showers. It was fantastic to be able to wash all the dried mud and sweat off, and it was great to share the camaraderie of the marines – they had all been training together for several months, and were completely used to seeing each other naked and being together in the showers. There was a lot of horseplay, as they had all finished for the day and were all in a good mood: I'd never known that men could be so much at ease with their own naked bodies and those of their mates, and it was good to be there in the warm spray of the showers with so many great guys around.

Afterwards, as they were dressing, I didn't know what to do as all I had to put on was my jockstrap, and it was now absolutely filthy from the mud on the assault course. One of the marines saw my dilemma, and came over with his own jockstrap that he'd taken off.

"Here, fellah, he said cheerily. "This one is soaked in my sweat, but at least it's not muddy. I can see you're all bandaged up down there – did they cut you this morning?"

I told him yes, and he went on "Well, you'd really better put this on then. They cut all of us, too, when we arrive at this base if we've not been done already – we may need to go undercover in covert operations in the Middle East, so they think it's better to cut us all, as standard. I know how irritating it is to have that great wadge of bandage around your dick – I can still remember when I had one – and if you don't support it properly it will be even worse."

He handed me his jock, and I could see that it was quite clean, except that as I took it in my hands it felt damp and clammy with his sweat. There was also a slight piss stain in the cup, just like the one I'd had to wear earlier – but then, I suppose all guys' underwear has that to a greater or lesser extent. I could see the sense in what he was saying ,though, and so I put aside my inhibitions and pulled the jock on. After the initial feeling of cold, it soon felt entirely natural.

The marine sergeant who had been in charge of the training saw me standing there, and deputised two of the men to take me back to my quarters. Dave wasn't in there, and I was so exhausted I simply collapsed across the bed and fell into a deep sleep.

It was the door opening, to let Dave in, that woke me, and he grinned at me and asked in an irritatingly cheery way if I'd had a good day. "Well," he replied, after I'd told him just how much every muscle in my body was hurting me, "It will get worse. We'll step up the exercise every day, as we need that body of yours in great shape. And there's some other, special training that I will give you – but we can't move on to that until that dick of yours is healed properly: we need to wait until the scabs have gone."

"I'm going to leave you here by yourself tonight as I have another mission on. You can watch the TV if you like, but all the channels are erotic: we want to get your mind thinking about sex all the time. If I were you, I'd lay off it tonight, though, as it's probably not good to have too many erections with your dick in the state it is."

I suppose he was right, and, anyway, I was completely and absolutely exhausted. He left me a few of the biscuits, which I was beginning to realise were going to be my only food, just as he'd said, and lapsed into a deep, deep sleep.

Part 5

This pattern of morning exercise in the gym and assault courses in the afternoon was repeated over the next five days. I only saw Dave occasionally, as he sometimes just dropped in to watch me for a few minutes now and then.

I went to the doctor's office twice to have the dressing on my dick changed, but he hardly spoke to me at all other than to say he was pleased with progress. The instructors basically just commanded me and shouted at me, and the marines I came into contact with mostly ignored me – they were a close-knit group, and had a lot of banter amongst themselves that I really did not understand, and could not join in with. All in all, I was pretty lonely and isolated, but it hardly mattered as the constant exercise left me so tired that as soon as I was back in my room at night all I really wanted to do was sleep. I tried to watch some of the TV, but, just as Dave had told me, it was all porn – and other than the channel we had watched on the first occasion, where there had at least been one woman involved, it was all about guys fucking each other! I really was not interested, and thought most of it was pretty vile.

My life changed radically on day six though, when I had been taken to the doctors, he had unwrapped my dick, and pronounced it "healed". Dave came in at that point, and he and the doctor had quite a discussion about my dick! I should have been as embarrassed as hell, I know – but after spending so much time totally naked, or wearing just a jock, it almost seemed natural. Dave told the doctor that he thought he had done an excellent job on me – the shaft of my dick was smooth and unblemished, and other than the change of skin colour where the cut had been, that's unavoidable, they agreed, it looked great.

Dave reached down and actually felt my dick whilst this conversation was going on! As he was talking to the doctor about the smoothness of the shaft, he was running his fingers up and down along it – I did the only thing any guy would do in the circumstances – I started to get an erection! Now I don't care how many times you get naked with other guys in the showers, there's one thing that guys just don't do together – they don't sport great hard-ons! So as I felt myself changing from soft to hard, I was really embarrassed – I went to stop Dave, by grasping his wrist with my strong hands, and the next instant I was writhing on the floor in agony.

Dave has prodded at me with a small cattle prod that he'd pulled from his pocket as I grasped his other hand. He stood there looking down at me, and said

"Steve, let that be a lesson to you! NEVER stop a master from doing whatever he's doing to your body. NEVER, OK?"

I was too out of control to do anything other than grunt, and he went on "Your master has the complete right to do whatever he wants with your body, and you must never prevent him from doing so. Indeed, you should be glad that you're still in training – some masters regard a slave who actually tries to prevent his master from touching him, by physically restraining the master, to be so wilful and disobedient that only the most sever punishment will suffice. Bear in mind that penalties such as the cutting off of the hand can be imposed: it's probably unlikely for a first offence, as you'll be an exceedingly valuable slave, but if your master was in a bad mood, who knows what he might order?"

"You've got to get over any feelings you might have had about your body, you know. It's not yours any longer – it actually belongs to your master. And if your master wants to fondle your dick, or show it to its best advantage to his friends by stroking you to erection, that's his choice, not yours."

I'd almost pulled myself together as he was talking, and managed to stagger to my feet. Dave approached me and again put his hand down to my dick. He was holding his cattle prod visibly now, and I therefore thought better of actually trying to prevent him. He stroked my dick, rubbing his thumb sensually along the shaft and letting it just catch the edge of the flange at the head on each stroke. I was soon completely erect – my dick had swelled out to its full size, and was curling upwards as his hand continued to move. I just stood there, rather amazed at what was happening to me, and I don't know how long this would have continued except that a more primitive force took over.

I hadn't been able to jerk off for days, ever since the operation, and so I guess my balls were just about aching for relief. As Dave continued to stroke me, I saw big drops of pre-cum start to appear on my dick head, and Dave obviously felt them too, as he stopped what he was doing and held his hand up and examined his fingers.

"So, Steve, all primed to fire, are you?" he said with a little smile. "Well, boy, hold in there. There'll be lots of opportunity for that later on!"

"As I said, doctor," he continued, "A really excellent job. Is he OK to use it now? I can see there is no more scarring, but is there any danger of the cuts opening up if he puts that dick to hard use tonight?"

"No, once the scabs have fallen off and the underlying new tissue is exposed, it's as strong as it will ever be. The boy can use his dick just as he did before... Why – do you have something planned for this evening?"

"Sure I do. As you can see, the physical training of his body is going well, but he's got another set of lessons to be learned before we can give him as a suitable gift from the people of the USA – he's got to learn all the arts of proper man to man sex, and, more importantly, to learn to enjoy it. He's never had proper sex, so there's a whole lot of teaching to do. You know how difficult it can be with some guys – they think they know it all, just because they can jerk themselves off and can fuck a woman. This one's just like that, so there's a whole way to go before we're done."

"Still," he continued, "With a body like this one has, and this splendid dick, the teaching should actually be a whole lot of fun!"

"Do you do it yourself?" the doctor asked.

"Mostly – especially in the early stages. But later on I use whoever's to hand: mostly some of the new marine recruits. But why do you ask? Are you volunteering your services?"

"No, but it's a thought! I've got several regular fuck buddies here on the base, but it would be good to have something new as a bit of a change every now and then. Especially when it's got a splendid body like this one."

"Are you top or bottom, doc?"

"Top. So if you need someone to plough that ass of his..."

"I'll remember that, doc. Thanks for your help so far."

Whilst they had been talking I had been listening with mounting horror to what they were saying. What was all this about "training". And could the doctor really be serious about fucking me? Indeed, was I going to have to learn to take a man up my ass? It sounded disgusting, and I would have started to argue with Dave and the doctor, except that Dave was waving his cattle prod around as he was speaking, and I knew that he wouldn't hesitate to use it on me. I decided, on balance, to keep quiet, and see what happened.

Dave shook hands with the doctor, and snapped at me "Come on, Steve. Let's get back to our room. The sooner we give you some relief, the better, if you ask me."

I went to put the jock strap back on that I'd been wearing when I'd gone in to the doctor, but Dave told me not to bother "You've lost that bandage from around your dick now, so there's no need. And, anyway, aren't you proud of your 'new look'? Don't you want to show it off to everyone we meet?"

Actually, no I didn't! I hated being naked and being looked at by the guards and the other marines who were in the corridors. And to make it worse, my erection just wouldn't go away – as hard as I tried, I just couldn't think of anything that was so un-sexy that it would collapse.

Dave had opened the door now and was going out into the corridor, so I had to follow. You know ho it is when you try to walk with an erection – your dick feels so heavy as it thrusts out in front of you, and it sways from side to side in time with your steps. I don't think I've ever been so embarrasses as I was now as we strode along – I could actually see one or two of the guards smirking at the sight of me fully on display like this. I felt there must be a steady stream of pre-cum leaking from me, too, as I know I'm very copious like that. In my imagination – and I'm sure it must have been my imagination as the breeze as we moved along would make it impossible – I even thought I could smell the pre-cum, and knew that the other guys would be smelling it too!

The walk seemed to go on for hours, I was so conscious of being looked at, but it was probably no more than three minutes before we were again in "our" room.

"So, Steve... You look ready to shoot!" Dave told me. "So why don't you do just that. Jerk yourself off, and get rid of all that accumulated tension. I know what it must fell like not to have been able to jerk off for six days!"

I went to go into the bathroom, but Dave rapped "Have you forgotten lesson one already? On your first night I taught you the correct way of doing it when your master commands you to cum. If you're not going to learn, you'll be getting a whole lot of tastes of my cattle prod. Now, cast your mind back – remember the position, and do it properly."

Knowing that I had very little choice, as Dave not only had the cattle prod but could also call the marine guards in, I started to do as I had on that first day. I fell to my knees, and spread my knees apart, pressing my feet together. Keeping my body upright, I rocked back until my ass was resting on my heels, then I reached down and started to stroke myself.

It felt so different without my foreskin – I was used to having a whole lot of natural lubrication as the foreskin slid backwards and forwards over my dick head, and now there was nothing, other than my hand. The hard work I usually did, and all the exercising of the past few days meant that my hands are always rather rough and I have hard patched of skin at the base of my fingers from gripping tools, and the gym apparatus. I could feel these most distinctively now as my hand stroked the shaft of my dick.

"You can spit on your hand to lube it a bit, you know," Dave said to me by way of encouragement, and so I did. With my dick slicked with my spit I soon felt the unmistakable sensation of starting to cum, and naturally stopped stroking.

"Don't forget," Dave shouted, "Catch the cum with your other hand! We don't want a mess all over the floor."

I shot a huge load – my balls had been storing it for days. The palm of by big hand was completely full, and it was difficult to stop the cum pouring over the edge and escaping. The smell of it rose up to my nose as I continued to kneel there, feeling my heart pounding and letting my breathing return to normal.

Dave told me to get to my feet, and came and stood in front of me. I felt really stupid standing there, naked, with one hand full of cum. To my utter amazement Dave reached out and put his thump and forefinger into the pool of cum in my hand. He squeezed them together, and pulled them out, bringing a little tread of my cum along with it.

"Right, Steve. Fell better now? You're going to cum a lot more tonight, but it's as well to get all that accumulated stuff out of the way first – we want long, slow training sessions, and it will be much easier if you're not wanting to shoot all the time. You've got good cum, though – very thick and viscous, and a good quantity. I'm sure your new master – no, perhaps we'd better call him your new owner, as that's what he will be – will be pleased with it."

I was blushing all over now. The red heat had started somewhere on my shoulders and was now up my neck and all over my face.

"Come on, Steve, don't look so miserable and embarrassed," Dave continued. "It's perfectly natural and normal to cum, you know. And let's remember that all 100% of the male race jerks itself off from time to time. I do it, you do it, I know you do it, you know | do it... There's nothing to be ashamed of."

"Yes, but I've never done it in front of another guy before."

"Well, you have now. And you will do many, many more times in your life. So, let's move on to lesson two. Here's a question for you... When a slave has just cum, at his master's command, as you just have, what does he do with the cum?"

I had absolutely no idea. I supposed you'd want to get rid of it, so I replied "Go and wash it down the sink, Dave?"

"No! He waits to hear what his master wants him to do with it. Sometimes the master will want the slave to use the cum to lubricate the slave's ass and the master's dick, to make the experience of the master fucking the slave even more pleasurable and sensual than it would otherwise be. And sometimes the master will want to 'harvest' the cum, to use in breeding new slaves. But usually the mater likes to watch the slave dispose of it neatly and tidily, by lapping it up. And, this time, that's what I want you to do – bring that handful up to your face, and slurp it down, then lick your fingers clean."

I just couldn't! Other than on that first occasion when I'd been freshly brought here, I'd never tasted cum before, and the thought still appalled me. The first time I'd managed to do it as there wasn't very much – but now there was this great pool of the stuff in my hand. There was no way I could get all that down me without gagging and choking.

"Come on, Steve... Get a move on. Just bring your hand up to your mouth, put out your tongue and lap it up," Dave snapped. "And you'd better start to look as if you're enjoying it, too. No master wants to see a miserable looking slave – pretend it's a real treat for you, even if it isn't."

I could see him fingering the cattle prod, and knew I had no choice, really, so I did as I had been told. Like the first time, I was surprised at the taste – not at all as I had imagined from the smell. And once I had overcome my initial repugnance and taken a tiny exploratory sip, I was able to take it all down, and lick my fingers clean, without too much trouble.

Dave had been standing really close to me whilst this was going on, and then he did something that completely caught me off my guard: he took a pace forward, put his hand behind my head, pulled his face to mine, and kissed me on my lips. I was so amazed by this that as his tongue was forcing itself at me I responded reflexively by opening my mouth.

Now our tongues were beating together, and his hot breath was pushing in and out of me. It seemed to go on for ever, but in truth it could only have been for a few seconds.

Dave pulled away. "So, Steve... An experienced kisser. You've done this before, haven't you? And doesn't that cum in your mouth make it even better? I always like to kiss a guy when he's just got, or just had, a mouthful of cum."

"I... I... Well, obviously I've kissed a lot. But... But women. I've never kissed another guy before."

"Well, it's not all that different, is it? Two mouths, two tongues..."

"Yes... But... But..."

"But what, Steve?"

"Well, it isn't natural, is it?"

"And what's not natural about it?"

"Well, two guys..."

"Ah, I see. The big 'hetero' myth! Something is OK if a man and a woman do it, but it's not OK if two guys do it. Is that what you mean?"

"Yes, I suppose it is."

"Well, Steve, you'll soon learn differently, from practical experience. Let me give you a piece of useful advice, advice I've learned from working with lots of so-called 'straight' guys like you."

"Put aside your preconceptions, and just experience it! You'll soon find that there are all sorts of things that two or more guys can do together that are unbelievably pleasurable, and completely natural. It's only silly propaganda, put about by the 'breeders', that says it's in some way 'unnatural', or 'wrong'. You'll soon get to understand, I hope, that things that give the two guys so much pleasure can't possibly be wrong. Anything – and I mean anything – that two guys agree to do together is entirely natural and normal – it's only years of conditioning that have made you think otherwise."

"Now," he went on, "Let's try again."

He leaned forward, and again used his hand to pull my head towards his. This time I was prepared, and as his lips touched mine I resolutely didn't open them. Steve persevered for a moment or two trying to force my mouth open with his tongue, but then broke away.

"Look, Steve, I don't want to have to hurt you. But I have a lot of training to get through, and I need your willing co-operation for some of it. So stop being stupid, and try. Now, I'm going to do it again, and just go along with it. If you resist, I'll give you a burst of the prod."

He moved his head closer to mine, and started to kiss me. I felt his moist warm lips on mine, but I just couldn't bring myself to open my mouth. But a great burst of pain caused me to do so – Dave hadn't used the prod, but had instead reached down and given my balls a little twist. You know how it is if there's any suggestion of damage to your balls – your whole body goes into a kind of spasm and you go to cry out. As I did so, Dave's hot, wet tongue at once snaked in. It was amazing, actually – once I'd got used to the idea, it seemed perfectly natural to respond and I felt my own tongue starting to probe his mouth, almost as if my reflex.

My hand went around his head, too – it seemed to be the right thing to do – and our heads thrashed together in response to the ways in which our tongues were moving. I was breathing hard, and I could feel his hot breath on my face, too. I was acutely conscious of the feel of his clothes scraping along my naked body as we got closer and closer together.

After what seemed like ages, we broke away.

"See!" Dave said. "I think you found some of that VERY natural, didn't you?"

Actually, |I did. It felt right. Instead of worrying about what the girl was going to do, and having to make all the running, having Dave kiss me like that was a real change. And the feeling of his rough face and stubble against mine was exciting, somehow. I knew I didn't have to worry about crushing him or hurting him – I could pull him close to me as hard as I wanted, as he was another strong man who could resist if he wanted to, or go along with me.

"Actually, it did feel natural – except for being naked! I'm not used to feeling clothes on the outside, so to speak – when I have a woman, we're usually naked together!"

Dave grinned, and began to strip his clothes off – as usual, he seemed to think this was perfectly OK. The last time this had happened there had been quite a big bedroom with two double beds, and even then I'd been aware of the strangeness of the situation: two men naked together in a hotel room, rather than somewhere like a public changing room. But now he was then standing in front of me as naked as I was, and the whole atmosphere was even more heavily charged – we'd been kissing, and the room was so much smaller, and so much more obviously a bed room.

"OK, Steve, Again!" he said.

This time when we kissed he not only pulled my head to his, but with his other arm he pulled our bodies together. It felt so good – his hard warm flesh against mine, and I responded by wrapping my arm around his back and hugging him close, too. It was do different from kissing a woman – our bodies were together so much more naturally, without breasts intruding. And I could feel his dick against mine – we were both erect – and the patch of hair on his chest. As we struggled to get even more of each other in close contact with the other, I thrust my leg in-between his and got a tingle of excitement at the way the hairs on his legs brushed against mine.

I never thought it was possible, as I'd never fancied another guy, but obviously my body knew differently because my dick was hard as a rock, even though I'd only just cum. It was almost painful, it as straining so much. And I could feel that Dave's was in the same state as mine, as it pushed against the hard muscles of my belly. This was a new sensation, too – having my dick pressed hard up against hot flesh and, feeling a dick against me – I reached down and grappled around and tried to get more comfortable, not caring that I was touching and caressing Dave's intimate parts.

Dave moved backwards slightly and reached down, too, and kind of pulled our dicks together. I felt the warmth of Dave's dick all along the length of mine, and it was fantastic! His hand was trying to get around both dicks, and he started stroking us both: I'd never had another guy's hand on my dick before, either, and somehow the combination of Dave's hand and his dick was totally superb, totally right.

After a few seconds, Dave stopped stroking us and he shuffled a little. Then I felt his hands cupping my balls, as they hung down. Again, this is something I'd never known – another guy cupping your balls in his hot, moist palm (except the doctor at school, of course, but then he always put a latex glove on, and Dave's hand was so different).

We went on and on like this, kissing passionately and almost sucking the air out of each other, whilst grappling our bodies together as if we were trying to make them meld into one. I was fondling Dave's dick and balls and he was grabbing at mine, as we almost wrestled in our passion.

It was Dave who broke off, and we stood, only a pace apart, both our chests heaving as we sucked in air. Sweat was breaking out from both of us.

"So, Steve... You're quite a passionate one, aren't you?"

I just looked, as I didn't like to admit it.

"That's good. Your owner will want you to respond willingly and passionately, and after I've trained you, you'll be able to do that throughout whatever he commands."

"Now," he went on, "We need to move on, though, as there's a lot to do and not all that much time. Kneel down!"

I looked at him uncomprehendingly. What did he mean?

"Are you deaf, or stupid? KNEEL DOWN. Kneel, now, in front of me."

Yes, he did mean it. I hated the idea of kneeling in front of a man, but Dave, I knew, held all the cards – the cattle prod was lying on the chest near us, and the guards were only a call away.

"Just as there's a position for jerking off when you're ordered to, so there's a position for kneeling. You have your knees about a foot apart, so that your tackle can swing freely between your thighs. Feet together. Back straight. Hands neatly clasped behind your back, resting on your ass."

I shuffled to get in to the position he'd said.

"Now, the only other thing is the position of the head. Normally, if your master told you to kneel, you'd bow your head, to look properly subservient, with your eyes looking at the floor about three feet in front of you. But if your master is naked, and either obviously sexually excited as I am now, or looking as if he wants to piss, then you turn your face up and look up at him. Your eyes should be focused on his dick, but you should also be able to look at his face so that you can pick up on any non-verbal signals he is sending about your required conduct."

I did as he'd said, and Dave's big, fat, circumcised dick seemed to be enormous as it was almost at eye level. Dave moved a little closer to me, and I started to smell something I've now smelled so many times now, but was then totally new to me – that special scent of a man's dick, balls, and inner thighs: you all know it, so I need hardly describe it. That smell of musk, and the special sweat that gets secreted from the sweat glands around the crotch, all mixed with heady overtones of piss and pre-cum. Although I knew that I produced that smell myself, it hadn't occurred to me that other men did, too – you don't talk about that to other guys, do you? And my nose had never been near another man's named crotch before for me to find out.

"OK, Steve. The next lesson is all about taking your master's dick and pleasuring him by mouth."

"No... I can't..."

"You couldn't kiss a man a few minutes ago! Now, trust me, not that you have any choice. Man cock is one of the most sensual, most special things that you can take in your mouth. Now... "

Dave had taken another step forward and the tip of his dick was almost touching my lips. I thought he was going to push it at me, but instead he gripped it near the root, and started to swing it from side to side. He thrust his hips forward, and his hot dick was slapping each side of my face. It didn't hurt, but somehow the sheer humiliation of it was more than I could bear – I reached up and went to stop him."

"NO!" Dave shouted. "You keep your hands behind your back. Now... Put them back there, or else I'll have the marines come in and cuff you."

He carried on swinging his dick so it slapped at me, and I slowly, and reluctantly, moved my hands back.

Still gripping it by the root, Dave now stopped the swinging, and moved forward. Pre-cum was leaking out of his piss slit, and I could smell it as he got closer. Then the touch of his dick head came to my lips, and Dave gently played it along and back, so that I could feel the pre-cum sliming me.

"Good boy," he whispered. "Now, slowly and gently, open your mouth, and put your tongue right out."

"No... I can't..."

"Yes, you can, and you will! Now – do as I say – open your mouth, and tongue out."

I don't know whether it was the male scent flooding my nostrils that overwhelmed my usual reactions, the general subservience of my position, or the realisation that I might as well let the inevitable happen, but I slowly parted my lips. Dave inched himself forward, and I felt his hot dick touch the end of my wet tongue.

If I'd been asked in advance, I'd have told you that I would have recoiled in horror at having a dick anywhere near my tongue. But as it touched me, I got the first taste of Dave: his dick, his pre-cum, his sweat – all the taste buds on my tongue started to send me flavours I'd never experienced before.

"Stay calm, and perfectly still," Dave commanded, and he moved his hips gently backwards and forwards so that his dick ran along my tongue, and back.

"Now lean forward slightly, open really wide, and take my cock in," Dave hissed. "Be careful, though, no teeth! Just close your lips around my cock for now..."

Actually, far from hating it, I wanted to do it – it seemed just the right thing to do. My own body was responding with a huge erection and I knew I must be leaking pre-cum, so powerfully could I feel my dick straining for action.

I slid my lips backwards and forwards along the first inch or so of Dave's dick – I tried to get more in, but started to gag slightly and so backed off. Then, experimentally, I pulled back so that it came out of my mouth, and instead licked it all around the head, almost tickling the meaty flange with the tip of my tongue. I became more and more excited, and my licking turned into nuzzling, and I pressed my face forward, wanting to bury my nose into Dave's pubic region and suck his scent deep down inside me.

"Good boy. Good boy," Dave was saying, encouraging me. "Now take my cock back in..."

I opened my mouth again and leaned forward, and started to slide backwards and forwards over his hard shaft, revelling in the warmth and the taste of it. I became more and more excited, and wanted to show Dave how much I was enjoying it, so I almost pulled at him, and felt his flange scrape on my teeth.

There was a stinging blow, and I almost toppled over! Dave had quickly pulled completely out of me, and had swung at me and slapped me – very hard – on the side of the head with his open palm. My face was bright red, my ears were signing, and it hurt!

"I told you to be careful with the teeth! Some masters like having their cocks gently nibbled, but I don't. I told you not to let your teeth touch me. You're lucky you have me as a teacher – some masters get VERY cross indeed if so much as a tooth scrapes along them. I've seen slaves who have had all their front teeth forcibly removed by their masters because they have been incapable of sucking dick properly – I don't think there's much chance of that happening to you yet as no master would want to disfigure your handsome face, but you'd better be aware of it: as you get older, and your handsomeness fades, a master might decide to turn you into a toothless cock sucker if you fail to take proper care of him!"

"Now, boy, get back on my cock!"

I reached forward, and started to gently slide it in and out.

"Good, Steve... Good... Now hold on – keep those hands behind your back... And don't worry... Just hang in there..."

Dave's hands went behind my head, and suddenly he was pulling me towards him, at the same time thrusting forward violently with his hips. More of his dick that I wanted to take was being rammed in and out of my mouth, and I started to gag and choke. Dave's pulling and thrusting got harder and more violent, and I felt myself choking... There was nothing I could do... I couldn't help it... I reached out and started almost clawing at his legs and ass, trying to get away from him.

He stopped, and pulled out of me completely. I knelt there, choking and gagging, with a big stream of drool falling out of my mouth. I was wheezing and coughing almost uncontrollably.

"I told you to keep your hands behind your back! Do I have to have you cuffed?"

"I can't... I can't... I can't take you all down – you're hitting the back of my throat... I'm choking."

"Yes, of course you are. That's what I want. Sometimes a master likes to be sucked by the slave gently, as you were doing, playing his lips up and down his master's dick but concentrating on the dick head, because that's where all the sensation comes from. But sometimes the master will want a "throat fuck" – so that he gets his pleasure from the stimulation the slave's throat causes to his dick head. That often indices gagging and choking in the slave, even with a lot of training, most men can't fully suppress it. And, anyway, if your master is extremely powerfully hung, he can get so far down your throat that the air passage is blocked, and you start to pass out! Imagine that, Steve, feeling consciousness fading because a giant dick is blocking your throat... You will experience that later in the training, as we like to turn out men who at least know what to expect."

"However, for now....," he went on, "Get your hands behind your back, and get that mouth back on my cock!"

He let me slide gently up and down on him for what seemed like several minutes, and I guess that got him very close to cumming. But then he was pulling me to him with fresh vigour, and really thrusting at me – I started to gag and choke again, but there was no let up – he held on to my head and pushed harder and harder. Fortunately he shot almost immediately, and I felt his cum hitting the surfaces of my mouth and throat.

Dave pulled out, and stood there looking down at me. I could see his chest rising and falling with the heavy breathing he was doing, and a big trail of slime – probably a mixture of my spit and his cum – hanging down from the end of his dick. I stopped choking, and looked up at him.

I had that taste in my mouth. That taste I had only had just before, but with a difference – it wasn't my cum, it was another man's cum. In my mouth. One part of me felt disgusted. Another part of me was half agreeing with what Steve had said earlier – it did seem to be almost natural.

I hated being on my knees, subservient to another man. But his cum was OK!

Part 6

Dave continued to stand over me, with the remains of his cum forming a small trail hanging out of his piss slit.

"Clean me up, Steve." He commanded.

Although I had just taken a huge mouthful of his cum, the idea of voluntarily licking his cock again was almost repugnant to me.

He saw my evident distress, and sounded kinder. "Steve, you've got to learn! I thought you had begun to understand that anything two men could to do together is OK. Giving and taking cum is one of the most fantastic things that two men can do for each other. And caring for your master's dick is one of the ways of showing him that you understand that you are his slave. You may use your hands – take my cock, and gently clean the remaining cum from it with that tongue of yours: I know it's very prehensile, delightfully warm, and wonderfully slobbery. Now... Get to it... I'm tying to be patient with you as you're still learning, but there are limits to my patience, you know..."

What real choice did I have? I reached up, and took his dick in my hands. Even though he had just shot, he was still semi-erect, and I felt its hot strength between my fingers. Holding his dick very gingerly, I moved my face forwards and slowly and carefully licked his head clean of the remaining drops of cum – I almost couldn't taste them at all now, after the flood that I had taken such a short time ago.

"Good... Good boy." Dave leaned down and ruffled his fingers through my hair, rather as you would pet a dog that had pleased you.

"Right.. Let's move on. I've got to advance you a lot through the programme today. Get over and lie on the bed."

I scrambled to my feet and went and lay on the bed, on my back, feeling very apprehensive. Dave came over and lay beside me, then turned towards me and gestured for me to turn to face him. He locked his legs around mine, put one arm around my shoulders to pull my head towards his, then started to kiss me. As he did so, I felt his hands probing at my genitals, and then the warmth of him as he began stroking my dick. He moved to reposition himself and moved his legs around mine. Locking us even more closely together. He carried on kissing me, and his tongue probed in and out of me almost in time with his gentle stroking, and somehow everything began to synchronise – the movement of our bodies, the incessant passion of his tongue in and out of my mouth, the stroking of my cock, and our breathing. I began to experience strange feelings sweep through me – feeling s of wanting this man to be even closer to me, to feel even more of his warm, moist body against mine. I threw my arms around him, and began to hug him closer to me, and to my surprise, almost heard my self beginning to give little groans of pure pleasure – animal noises that originated somewhere deep down in my chest, and which I couldn't help making.

Dave's stroking of my cock became faster, and harder – he was squeezing his fingers together, so that as the flange of my cock head hit them, it gave me a little jolt of pure pleasure. Occasionally he stopped stroking and instead rasped his thumb nail over my cock head – I've been told that after you've been circumcised your cock head loses sensitivity, but mine was still "fresh" and wasn't used to being exposed and touched in this way, as it had always been protected from friction against my clothes by my foreskin. At the same time he was using his other hand to press a finger and thumb in to me at the base of my cock, just at the top of the ball sac – it was if he was probing for something.

And then he found it – a wave of pleasure shot through me, and it was so intense that my body went to jerk backwards away from his. At the same time, I gave a little cry of pleasure – or was it pain? You know how it is – if you've got a sensitive cock and you carry on jerking yourself after you've begun to shoot, there's that almost indescribable sensation of pain mixed with pleasure.

I felt myself beginning to pump out sperm – there was nothing I could do to stop it – and an enormous load of cum flooded into the space between our two sweaty bodies. Most of it went on me, and I could feel its sticky warmth on my belly.

In spite of my cries, Dave continued to pump my cock and probe with his fingers, and the feelings of such intense pleasure were definitely turning almost to ones of pain – I shouted, I begged, I laughed, I almost cried... I really don't know what I was saying, I was so completely overcome by it all.

Then he stopped, and we lay there, face to face, his shining eyes looking directly into mine.

"Enjoy that, Steve?"

"Oh, yes!"

"As good as you give yourself, when you jerk yourself off?"

"Fucking amazing – I didn't know jerking off could be like that!"

"Better than any hand job you've ever had from any of the whores you've slept with...?"

I had to admit it was.

"There you are – look at what you've been missing all these years! If you'd put aside your silly prejudices against sex with other men, you'd have found a few guys at school and experimented on each other – you could have been enjoying sex like this ever since you were old enough to first shoot off. A lot of men don't realise that being jerked off by another guy is so much better than doing it themselves – although I shouldn't be surprised, really. After all, some men still think that masturbation is some sort of sin, so it's not surprising that more guys don't get together to experiment and find out. Men will play team sports, go the gym together, go for a night out with the boys at a bar... But, amazingly, they won't try with another man the thing they know gives them so much pleasure: if they're willing to bond with other men in all these other ways, it escapes me as to why they don't try mutual masturbation."

"Anyway," he went on, "You've got to be taught how to probe for the prostate externally as well as internally, so that you can bring that intense pleasure to your master, if he wants you to jerk him off. We need to move on... I wanted that fresh load of cum from you as I want to lube and massage your asshole as I'm going to fuck you – you are a virgin, aren't you?"

"No – I've had a lot of sex... with a lot of women..."

"In this context, 'virgin' means that your ass has never experienced the pleasure of another man's cock. Since you'd never even touched another guy before you were brought here, I suppose I should assume no one has ever been up you...?"

"No... Please, Dave... Please don't fuck me. It's been bad enough when I've had to have a rectal exam at the doctor's... Please don't make me take anything up there. It's not right... A man's ass isn't meant..."

"Cut it out, Steve! Not another one of your curious ideas about what parts of a man's body can and can't be used for! You didn't think another guy could jerk you off and cause so much pleasure until a few moments ago, did you? So why don't you think it's right for a man's cock to go up you?"

"Well, the bible..."

Dave almost laughed. "That's just a load of superstitious nonsense written to keep the poor subservient to the rich, and to prevent people having fun!"

"Yes, but God says sodomy is wrong..."

"Oh Steve, you're so naive! Firstly, the bible was written by men, not by a God or Gods, even assuming you believe in such nonsense. Prejudiced men. And it forbids a lot of things, and pronounces on matters that are considered barbaric these days. For example, do you know what the punishment for adultery it prescribes is? You do know what adultery is, don't you? It's when you've been fucking those women, and they happen to be married. What do you think the bible says is suitable punishment for adultery?"

"I don't know."

"Stoning! You should be stoned to death! You don't believe that, do you?"

I shook my head.

"Well then, if the bible says sodomy is wrong, why do you believe that?"

"Well, I don't know, I suppose..."

"And, as I said, it was all written by men anyway. Even if you do subscribe to the big juju in the sky theory, why on earth would it want to prevent you from having fun with your friends?"

"But it's not fun... It's disgusting... It hurts... "

"Look, Steve, trust me! It is fun – whole loads of fun – just like wanking another guy is fun. It's not disgusting – how can anything that two men do together be disgusting? It need not hurt, if you're properly prepared and relaxed – although, of course, some men do like to hurt when they fuck, and some men like being hurt as it enhances their pleasure."

"Think about these two things," he went on: "What's the biggest, fattest turd you've ever dropped? You can't be all that dissimilar to other men, and most men have shat turds that are far, far bigger than any cock ever is. So if a big, fat turd can get out, a cock can get in. And why do you think that the asshole is so perfectly engineered to take a cock – that can't just be by chance, can it? Evolution must have arranged it that way – it's meant to happen! All the muscles so that the cock can be squeezed to give additional pleasure; the nerves there, to send waves of pleasure through you; and, of course the way a cock is made – stiff, hard, like a ramrod, to be able to drive its way in."

"So there – now, let's stop talking about it, and let me show you."

Dave wiped his fingers in my cum that had shot all over my belly, and told me to lie on my back. He came and knelt by my waist, and then, looking intently into my eyes, reached between my legs – he kind of pushed them apart to give him access. I felt his finger probing for my ass hole, and then incessantly pushing, to go in. I squeezed my butt muscles, to try to stop his probing, but he said calmly and authoritatively

"Just relax, Steve. It's going to happen anyway – so just relax, don't tense up. Trust me..."

I tried, and soon felt his finger enter my sphincter. Then he slid it in and out gently a few times, sliding on the slickness of my own cum.

"OK?" He half whispered. I kind of nodded and mumbled OK.

Now his finger was circling around, and I was getting little sensations of pleasure from my hole. It was warm in the room, and I was somehow comfortable in Dave's presence, as his muscled body bent over me as he worked away.

I grunted as a second finger pushed gently at me to join the first.

"See, Steve... It's good, isn't it? You've relaxed, and now you've got two of my fingers up inside you. That means I can now..."

I really grunted now, as Dave's simple in and out sliding changed into something I could feel recognisably as "stretching" – he was forcing his fingers apart and I could imagine my hole being widened and opened.

It went on and on. And Dave was right – if I relaxed, it did make it easier. It became pleasurable, too, as Dave worked away, little drops of sweat from him occasionally dropping on to me.

Another grunt from me, and more stretching – I did try to relax, but it was hard to do so.

"That's three fingers," Dave told me. "Stay calm, Steve... Just lie and enjoy it."

Dave was obviously enjoying it as he cock had sprung a huge erection as he knelt there beside me, massaging my hole. He was so intent on what he was doing that he didn't notice how his cock would occasionally touch my body, along my hip or thigh, and I knew the erotic pleasure of having another man's proud cock against me – a cock that he was so unaware of, as he was intent on his other activity. This is the way that men should be together, I thought – naked, relaxed ,warm, and unconcerned for their bodies.

Dave stopped massaging and stretching me, pulled all his fingers out, and knelt upright, looking down at me. He reached and scraped the remaining drops of cum (now mixed with my sweat) from my ridged belly, and sensuously used them to slick his cock – I could see it, erect in front of him, glistening slightly in the room lights. A small bead of pre-cum was trailing from his piss slit, and Dave was breathing hard – surely not just from his exercise... It looked more as if he was very excited and turned on.

He shuffled around on the bed until he was kneeling between my legs, then picked each up in turn and put them on his shoulders. He shuffled forward more, so that I could feel the radiated heat from his loins striking my exposed crack.

"OK, Steve – this is it! Your initiation to real manhood. Reach down and pull your balls up and out of the way – a guy with very low hangers like you needs to keep them out of the way as his master goes to fuck him."

"For the first time it's actually easier to fuck a guy who's kneeling down," he went on, "or stretched across the side of the bed. But I think the first time is very important – you'll always remember it, and I want you to remember me. So I'm taking you like this, on your back, so that I can watch your face as I enter you. And I want you to look at me as I fuck you..."

"Now... Keep relaxed, keep calm..."

Dave shuffled forward on his knees again, and I felt something touch my exposed ass hole – something warm and moist – Dave's cock head. I tried to get away from it, tried to shuffle up the bed a bit, but I couldn't really move as Dave was gripping his arm around my knees, holding my legs close to his body. I could feel the warmth of his chest against the back of my calves, and his wiry thatch of hair brushing my legs. He shuffled a little further forward, and his cock was now insistently pressing against my ass hole, the he gently moved his hips forward. His cock was pushing in to me...

In spite of everything Dave had said, in spite of all his preparations, I wasn't ready for this. Jerking another man off, even sucking his cock – those are the sort of things men can do together. But my years of "straight" conditioning had taught me that a man did not get fucked up his ass; it wasn't right; real men did not get fucked."

"No!" I shouted, and struggled to get away. I pushed Dave to one side, and then didn't know what to do. There was no way out of the room for me as Dave exited by shouting for the guards to open the door, as there was no handle on the inside. I just went and sat on the edge of the bed, cradling my head in my hands with my elbows on my knees.

"You stupid fucker!" Dave shouted. "I've gone out of my way to be nice to you. I've told you to relax, and I've spent all that time making it easy for you by massaging and lubing you. And this is how you repay me! The moment my cock gets near your hole you lose it, and start to act like some naughty school kid. What the fuck's the matter with you?"

"I'm sorry, Dave... It's just... Well... I can't bear the thought of being fucked."

"Shut the crap, Steve. Lie back down, and let's get on. Look at my cock..." He was standing in front of me now, and holding his cock by its root and thrusting his hips slightly forward so that it reared up massively in front of me. "Look at it, Steve, and know that it's going into you – all the way in. Now, lie back down!"

"No, I can't. Dave... Anything else... Please let me suck you again..."

"OK, don't say I didn't warn you! No more 'Mr Nice Guy' from me, Steve. You're going to take it, and you're going to take it hard, now."

His voice changed, and he called out "Guards – in here!"

The door opened and two marines came in. They were really big, tough guys – their khaki singlets showed off their bulging biceps and massive shoulders. Their belts around their combat pants only served to emphasise the narrowness of their waists and their flat, muscular stomachs. They were both tall – at least 6'3".

"Another reluctant one – pin him down, as usual, and grab his legs," Dave said.

One of the marines grinned, and said "Same as before, sir, we hold him for you, then we get him?"

"Of course!" Dave smiled at them. "Of course. One good turn deserves another."

The marines leapt at me, and I was overwhelmed. I couldn't put up much of a fight as they had big combat boots on and looked as if they would use them on my naked body if I resisted. But I didn't have much of a chance anyway – they hurled their hard bodies on me, throwing me backwards from where I was sitting on the edge of the bed. The next moment they'd pulled my arms out to the sides, and the marines were kneeling on me, each straddling a shoulder and my upper arms. As I moved my head in terror all I could see was their combat pants on either side of me, as they held me there. Their hard bony knees pressing in to me were hurting, and I tried to wriggle to get more comfortable, but it was no use – I was immobile beneath their weight.

Dave picked up my left leg and "handed" it to the marine kneeling on my left shoulder and arm, and he wrenched it back and tucked it neatly under his left arm. I felt the hot moistness of the marine's arm pit, with its thick forest of under arm hair, against my ankle. My right leg followed to the other marine, and I realised that I was now completely and humiliatingly exposed – pulling my legs back and apart had made me bend my waist slightly, and my ass was now quite high in the air with my hole fully visible to Dave as he stood there.

He didn't say anything, but climbed back onto the bed, positioning himself next to my ass.

"OK, guys, hold him tight – he'll be a real bucking bronco, I expect, as I'm going in hard."

"Yes, sir!" The marines chorused in agreement.

Dave raised himself up slightly so he was towering over my ass, pointed his cock slightly downwards, and drove down, aiming his cock at my hole.

This was no gentle pushing and careful sliding of his cock in to me as he'd been trying to do before – the whole weight of Dave simply pushed it hard and brutally into me. I shrieked as I was violated, not just because it hurt like hell, but because something inside me made me want to cry out at the indignity I was suffering. I tried to thrust my body upwards, sideways, any way to get it out from under Dave, but impaled on his cock, with the marines kneeling on my upper torso, I could no nothing. I just vaguely thrashed around.

Dave looked down at me. He had an evil smile on his face, and was breathing hard. As he watched me he moved upwards and then thrust down again, and I screamed again. He did it a third time, then a fourth.

He stopped again and now I could see sweat breaking out all over his body, to match that on mine.

"Enjoying it, Steve? Let this be a lesson to you – take the training and do as I say, or suffer the consequences. Now..."

Mercifully, he stopped the hard thrusts he had been doing and began to inch himself out of me, and then very gently lower himself back in. I started to feel a warmth, a glow, sweep over me. I could feel the heat of his slimed cock against my ass hole, and it felt good.

"The tits, guys," Dave said, and each marine reached down and started to twist and tweak my nipples. I wanted to buck upwards with the pleasure and that indescribable sensation you get when your nipples are played with. They were quite harsh, though, and I shouted once or twice at particularly hard tweaks that caused me real pain. All the time Dave continued his slow, rhythmic fucking of me, and I found myself quite unable to prevent myself starting to moan with pleasure, synchronising the deep animal sounds I was making to the movement of Dave in and out of me.

I wanted it to go on for ever – my breath was now coming in great gasps, and I was transported somewhere else. I looked up at Dave, and saw the intense look of sexual domination on his face as he thrust away. He too was covered in sweat now, and little drops of it were flying off his body and landing on mine.

He saw me looking up at him, and abruptly changed his stoke – a harsh thrust caused me to try to buck again, and my moans of pleasure turned into a cry of pure animal savage hate for him.

Dave went on and on, varying from the careful, slow, gentle thrusting one minute, to a couple of hard slams into me the next. I could feel his wiry pubic hair against my bare ass, and heard the "slap" as his belly and thighs hit against my ass. And all the time the marines carried on tweaking and twisting my nipples.

There were floods of sensation everywhere – my nipples were on fire, my ass was alternately revelling in pleasure and freezing with pain, and I'd lost conscious control of my voice – I heard myself, from a great distance, alternatively cursing Dave, begging him to go on, shouting "fuck, fuck, fuck" and "Oh God, Oh God" and making noises that must have come from my primeval past as I had no idea what they were.

Dave was still looking at me and I at him, and then I saw a new look come over him – he became grimly determined, and his stroke changed to one of very long, quite fast ones – in and out, in and out... But then it was all over. I heard Dave shout "Oh fuck... I'm cumming... Oh..." And then his body almost froze in mid air. I knew his cum must be pumping out into me, and he gave one or two little half strokes, as if trying to squeeze the last remaining bits of pleasure from the experience. Then he was still.

He was breathing hard, and the intense look on his face had been replaced by his normal cheerful smile.

"So now you're not a virgin, Steve. That's what sex with men is all about! Remember!"

He pulled himself upwards and out of me, got off the bed, and went through into the bathroom. The marines remained kneeling on me, and we listened as water ran in the bathroom – I guess Dave was washing my crap off his cock – there was a distinct look of brownness as he moved past me, and the faintest whiff of faeces in the air.

The marines had stopped playing with my nipples once Dave stopped, and as I looked up, I saw them lean towards each other and kiss. I didn't know marines did that, but as I lay there letting my thoughts drift and wondering what was next, I supposed it wasn't so strange – virile guys like that, always working and living with other men, it was natural they'd want to experience each other's bodies, wasn't it?

Dave came out of the bathroom, and motioned for the marines to get up. They scrambled off the bed, and stood there. I got up, too, and sat there looking at Dave. Dave didn't seem to be a bit concerned about having had those marines see him fuck me, and wasn't at all bothered now as he stood in front of them with his rapidly detumescing cock. I just didn't know how a man could let other men watch him perform this totally intimate act – I tried to imagine how it would have been for me if a couple of marines had wanted to watch me fuck one of my girl friends, but just couldn't – the effort was too great.

"Learn anything, boys?" He asked cheerfully.

"Uh, sir, I don't know, sir," one of them answered. "But is it time for us to find out now? You did say we could have a go, sir."

"Oh, sure. Any way you want – he's got a lot to learn, and most of it's new to him. So do whatever you like – but no permanent damage, OK?"

"YES, sir," the marines snapped.

They bent over and unlaced their boots, pulled them and their socks off, and undid the belt on their combat pants. Each of them stripped his pants off, followed by his regulation khaki jock strap, and stood there in his khaki singlet. They reached down and started to jerk themselves off, and I heard the little tinkling of their dog tags as their arms moved up and down.

Their erect cocks were on the same scale as the rest of them – big, and thick.

"Who's first? You want to take him first?"

"No, you can."

"OK."

This negotiation over, the one who had "won" looked at me.

"Right – are we going to have any more trouble, or shall we just have a quick, workmanlike fuck?"

He saw me hesitating. I still didn't want to be fucked.

He came up to me, pushed me towards the end of the bed, then snapped at me to lie down, my ass in the air and my feet on the ground.

"I think this one's still a struggler!" he told him mate, and the other marine leapt onto the bed, sprang astride me, and sat down on my back, just below my shoulders. I could fee his hot cock lying on my naked shoulder, and the warm moistness of his asshole pressing down on to my backbone. I knew there was no way I could get up, no way I could displace the weight of this big man.

Then I felt it again – that hot feeling, as a cock head touches the sensitive skin of your ass hole. The first marine was between my legs, and was about to enter me.

It was "workmanlike" – very little shouting, no passion, just a slow, rhythmic thrusting in and out of me that gradually got faster and faster and more and more intense. Then I heard him shout "Oh yes.. .fuck...," and everything stopped, and he pulled out of me.

"Do I need to hold him for you?" he asked his buddy, who had now climbed off my back and was standing there evidently waiting to start to fuck me. "He seems to have quietened down under my dick – I don't think you'll have any more problems."

"Better to be safe than sorry – anyway, he's a nice ride – good, hot sweaty back – it feels good under your asshole."

The marine who had just fucked me therefore climbed on the bed and straddled me – unlike his friend who had faced my head, he sat facing the guy who was going to fuck me. I could feel his ass almost pushing my neck down into the bed, and his very wet, slimy cock was lying neatly on my spine.

I was expecting the second marine just to start fucking, but I jerked as a mighty "slap" hit my ass – the guy was spanking me! I cried out, not just from the unexpectedness of it, but because it actually hurt – a big strong marine can really put some power behind his hand!

The blows reigned down, and I heard Dave shouting "Stop! I told you you were welcome just to fuck him, but that there was to be no damage!
"

"Sorry, sir! I thought he was just a bit unresponsive when Marine Simons fucked him. I like my men to wriggle and squirm a bit, so I just wanted to tenderise and sensitise his ass a little."

"Just get on with it, Marine. If you want to fuck him, just do it, whether he gives you the satisfaction of wriggling and squirming, or not. Do you want to empty that big ball sac of yours today, or not?"

"Yes, sir! Right away, sir!"

He wasted no time, and I felt his cock push at me. There was absolutely no resistance – he went straight in, and started fucking – although each time he fucked me hard, there was a tingle and shock from my tender ass as his pubic hair hit my tenderised flesh.

He was moaning, as I had been, and his friend was shouting encouragement – then they were both almost silent – I tried to turn my head, and couldn't rally, but in the bedroom mirror I saw that the one sitting on my shoulders was leaning forwards and had his arms locked with his buddy's. As the marine fucking me thrust away – I could see his big, strong ass muscles powering him in and out of me – the two were kissing each other passionately. I might as well not have been there – I was just being used as a receptacle for this man's cock, to bring some little additional pleasure to him as he made "proper" love to his buddy.

Once he had shot his load, the two marines went into the bathroom, and Dave sat on the bed, near my head. As we hard the marines laughing with each other as they washed their cocks, Dave said, in a low voice "OK, Steve?"

"No – I hurt!"

"Don't worry, there's no permanent damage. You're just a bit sore. Three big cocks, one after the other, and your first time, too... Perfectly normal. It will be a bit painful to crap tonight and tomorrow morning, but by tomorrow night you'll have forgotten all about it and you'll be ready to take me up you again. And this time, do as you're told, and I'll show you exactly how much pleasure it can be."

"Fuck you, Dave! You raped me!"

"You do want to be punished, don't you? How can it be rape? You no longer have any say in what happens to your body, as we discussed earlier. I control that, and if I want to push my cock down your throat or up your ass, it's not your choice. And, anyway, you've been really stupid – your first experience of full man to man sex could have been a lot of fun for both of us – as it was, it was only me that enjoyed it!"

The two marines had now come out of the bathroom, and had pulled their jockstraps, combat pants, socks and boots on. They too had seem to be unconcerned about stripping and fucking in front of Dave – perhaps men did this, after all. Perhaps I'd been too much of a prude all my life.

"Anything else, sir? Would you like us to hold him again?"

"No thanks, guys. Dismissed."

They went out, Dave told me to go into the bathroom to clean up, and then ordered me back into bed with him.

Part 7

I was so sore as I lowered myself gingerly on to the bed. I felt violated. I could feel the cum of Dave and the two marines trickling out of my ass hole. I could smell them all over me – the scent of their sweat where their bodies had pressed against mine, the taste of their spit in my mouth from their kissing, and of course the aroma from the cum which was everywhere in the room.

Dave came and lay beside me, pulled the sheets up over both of us, and turned out the light so that the room, which ha been bright – so bright that I could see the lights shining in the sweaty bodies of the men – was now almost dark.

"Get to sleep, Steve. Just because you've been fucked doesn't mean that you don't have to work tomorrow – we need to keep toning that body of yours."

I didn't want to say anything to him in reply. How could he have done this to me? It was so degrading, to have had him and those marines to take me so violently, so completely against my will, and taking away all my ability to resist them.

Dave son fell into a deep sleep – I could hear his breathing slow and deepen, and his body moved slightly as he settled himself comfortably into the bed. He threw an arm casually over me, so that we were pressed close – it was as if he wanted to possess my body, even as he slept. But I couldn't sleep – I kept going over and over in my mind what had happened to me. My cock was rock hard, too – for some reason I was in a state of extreme sexual arousal, so extreme that I was sweating, my body was actually hurting from the strain in my cock, and my mind was fantasising about the feel of flesh against me and the powerful thrill that fucking gave me.

Dave stirred again, and turned over in his sleep so that his ass was towards me. My cock went to nestle in his ass crack, and I could feel the sweaty moistness of his body against my member as it lay against him, gently straining every now and then as if it was trying to get even harder.

As I lay there, a plan began to form in my mind. I knew it would probably result in the most terrible punishment for me if I did it, but what did it matter – I could see that I was going to have not much of a life anyway as a "toy" for some Arab. So perhaps I should exert my manhood in one last attempt to show them that I was still a human being, still someone capable of taking independent action. The more I thought about it, the more I was determined to do it. I needed to prove that I was still a man.

I carefully slid away from Dave, lowered my feet to the floor, and gingerly stood up, all so that I should not disturb his sleeping. I found Dave's boxers where he had dropped them before fucking me, picked them up and moved to the end of the bed.

I stood there looking at the sleeping man as he lay there sprawled so casually, half on his side, half on his stomach, stretched out in that easy way that men have when they've been fucking. My heart was racing, and I was beginning to breathe hard. If I was going to do it, I had to act quickly and decisively. I seemed rooted to the spot, unable to act. I think if Dave hadn't half woken up and become aware of me standing there looking at me, I would probably have done nothing and gone back to bed.

As it was, Dave mumbled "Get back here, Steve. I want to feel your ass against my cock again..."

That was it! That was more than I could bear – being commanded like that to be used as a sex toy. I flung myself onto Dave, landing with a big "slap" as our naked bodies hit. He was so surprised and only half awake, and couldn't do anything. I had him in an arm lock, and my legs were wrapped around his. Even so he was trying to buck and struggle to get away from me, and before he could shout for the guards I pushed his head down – hard – into the pillow.

He was making muffled cries, but I reached and grabbed his balls, and gave them an experimental squeeze.

"Shut up!" I hissed at him, "Unless you want me to rip your balls off. Now... Shut the fuck up."

He stopped shouting, but I could feel his body was like a tense, coiled spring under me.

I allowed him to raise his head from out of the pillow, as I didn't want him asphyxiated.

"Open your mouth – I'm going to gag you with your boxers."

There was no response, so I gave his balls a little warning tweak. A brief gasp of pain from Dave, and he opened his mouth – he knew he had little choice! I balled up some of the cotton of his boxers and stuffed it into his mouth, then used by strong finger to force and cram as much more of them in as I could – I packed his mouth so tightly that there was no way he could spit them out, using my fingers almost like tamping rods to force the fabric in. Good! With that done, he couldn't call to the guards for help.

I let go of his balls, and he started struggling again, so I pinched his nose closed. At once, his body became frantic as he tried to thrash around to get away from me, and his hands were almost tearing at my muscular arms to try to break my grip.

"Lie still!" I commanded. "Lie still unless you want to die."

It must have taken a huge effort of will to relax, but I felt his body under mine go motionless, so I let go of his nose and he sucked in great drafts of air.

"Now listen, Dave... Any resistance and I'll hold your nose closed until you pass out – you can't breathe through your mouth at all. Or, of course, I might just hold it closed until you die."

I could feel both of us breathing hard as we lay there with me clamping his body close to mine. There was an incredible amount of sweat pouring off both of us, I remember feeling the bottom sheet of the bed sticking to my flanks as I shuffled around. I manoeuvred Dave's body so he was lying on his belly, under me, then used my feet to kick his legs apart. My cock was so hard I thought I was going to cum there and then, but I managed to restrain it as I moved my body down over Dave's so that my cock was forcing its way into his ass crack. It was tricky to keep my arm lock around Dave's neck whilst freeing my other hand to guide my cock, but I managed it somehow – the struggle and physical difficulty all added to my raging excitement, and I had anyway lost the power of all rational thought. All I wanted to do was complete my plan, and the sexual excitement from my cock and the totally abandoned nature of it all made my brain go into overdrive. It was as if someone had turned up all my senses- the rasping breathing from Dave and me, the thudding of my hearts, the smell of our sweat and the dried cum from earlier, and the sound of Dave starting to make moaning and whining noises all seemed as if they were bigger, better, louder, stronger than usual. Nothing else mattered. Nothing else intruded between us, nothing was going to stop me making this man bend to my will and take my cock deep inside him.

I managed to position my cock head, which was now leaking pre-cum everywhere, at the entrance to Dave's hole. I could feel its sticky moistness pressed against me, and the warmth it was radiating only inflamed my desire. I pushed down as hard as I could, and had it not been rock hard, I'm sure my cock would simply have bent as Dave was clenching his muscles and trying to prevent me getting in. I pushed harder and harder, and Dave was now writhing under me and his moaning and whining sounded frantic, although no recognisable sounds came out and there wasn't enough noise to alert the guards. Then there was that sudden jerk, that little acceleration of your body that I now always look for as you finally pop through the sphincter – I was in.

The sensation of his hot body, powerless under me, and the feeling of domination I had with my cock spearing his ass, was incredible. I wanted to throw back my head and give a great primeval shout about how I had vanquished my oppressor. There was no stopping me now – I thrust myself further in, quite brutally. There was a great noise from Dave, and I felt my pubic hair slam hard against the flesh of his ass as my cock went full in, as far as it would go.

Then I pulled out, and slammed in again, and again, and again. In spite of the gag, Dave was making a great noise, and I should have reached up and starved him of oxygen. But I didn't care – I was in charge, I was fucking this body. I was having sex like I'd never had it before. My passion had totally taken over, and I was doing what a real man does: taking my pleasure without concern for the other guy.

It seemed as if I was going faster and faster, harder and harder, as I fucked away, and I wanted it to go on for ever. But of course the inevitable happened, and I got that magic tightening feeling in my balls and the flood of new sensation to my brain as I started to cum.

I just had to stop thrusting in and out as a huge load of cum pumped into Dave – the sensations from my cock were so powerful that it was actually hurting if I tried to continue. I forced myself to go on as far as

I could, though, as this new, wonderful sexual pain was like a drug – I wanted more and more, but my body couldn't take it.

It had totally exhausted me. All I could do was lie against Dave, with the rivulets of sweat from us both causing little tingles of excitement all across my bare body. We were both breathing very hard, and Dave's cries of outrage, or pain, or whatever, had subsided. All he was doing was making little tiny deep noises from somewhere – almost as if he was crying.

I don't know how long I lay there like that – the feeling of having him impaled on my cock was so erotic, that I wanted it to go on for ever. But as I calmed down, I knew I had to face the consequences of my actions. So I gently moved my hips and allowed my cock to slide out, very gently, from his ass hole. At the same time, I pulled at the fabric of his boxers, and began to un-gag him.

The boxers were wet all over as they lay there beside his head on the pillow, and now I could hear Dave making little sobbing noises. I didn't know what to say, or do.

"You bastard! You raped me!"

"Yes. But you raped me earlier, and got those two marines to carry on."

"That's not the point! You are a toy, being trained. What we did to you was education, not rape. But you raped me – you forced yourself into me, when I didn't want it..."

"I didn't mean to...."

"You stupid cunt, Steve! Don't you get it yet? No one cares what you want or mean. It doesn't matter what you like and don't like. You're going to be given to an Arab friend of this country as a gift, a toy, something he can use to amuse himself with. But you raped me – you knew you shouldn't, and you knew I'd object – that's why you gagged me. And now I have to decide how to punish you."

"Ordinarily, I'd get the marines in here to beat the shit out of you, then have you tied down to a fucking table in the marine barracks, and let it be known that I expect the whole squad to use you. I might also order you to lose a testicle, or even go for full castration. But I don't have that choice – I have to hand over a good looking body, not something battered and broken. And I expect your new owner will want a whole man, in case he decides to use you for stud, or, perhaps, wants to take your balls off himself. But you've got to be punished, and punished in a way that will constantly remind you that you are a toy, something that is used, and that you never instigate action."

To tell you the truth, I didn't care. I'd proved myself still to be a man. And I'd had such an amazing experience – the sexual rush I'd had in fucking Dave had beaten anything I'd ever experienced with any of the women I'd been with.

Dave now shouted "Guards!" And the marine guards burst into the room.

"Take this and put it in a cage until tomorrow," he rapped. "I've got to talk to the State Department and see what we can do with him."

The marines came towards me, and the one in charge said "Are we going to have any trouble with you?"

I answered him by trying to push past him and run out of the door. I had no idea what I'd do then – but I wanted to do something, make some gesture.

I had no chance, of course. The other marine just stuck his booted leg out, and I went flying over it. The other one threw himself onto me as I lay on the floor, and it literally "knocked the wind out of me,"

"You want to fuck it again?" Dave asked the marines.

"Thanks, sir, but no. We've just jerked each other off, and I don't think we could make it. But thanks for the offer – it was a good fuck last time." As he'd been speaking, the marine had pulled my arms behind me, and I felt the cold steel of cuffs being put on me.

"On your feet!" he rapped at me. And of course that's not easy – when you're winded, and cuffed, getting up off the floor is a problem, but in spite of the physical difficulty, I decided to do nothing anyway, as a protest.

"Get up off the fucking floor," the marine snarled when he saw I was ignoring him. "If you're not on your feet in ten seconds you'll feel my boot in your balls."

I could see he wasn't joking – his combat boots were on the same level as me, and he was a big, meaty guy. Although Dave had said I wasn't to be damaged, I didn't like to take the risk that the marines knew that. So I scrambled upwards, and stood there.

"Follow me!" the marine rapped, and I decided to carry on my protest by simply ignoring him. I just stood there. I expected he would threaten me again with a good kicking, but he just shrugged slightly, came close to me, and grabbed hold of my cock. He used it as a sort of "handle" to pull me along after him, out of the room, and down the corridor. Of all the humiliations I'd already suffered here at this training base, this was the worst! I was just an object to them, just something to be "handled" in the easiest way possible for them. The marine wasn't getting any thrill from holding my cock, he was just using it as it was most convenient for him.

We went along a number of corridors, with the marines keeping up a fast pace, but we didn't go out of the building we were in. It's difficult to walk quickly anyway when you're cuffed, but when a guy is leading you by pulling on your cock, it's almost impossible. I had to take little quick short steps to keep up with them, and almost stumbled several times.

"Careful!" the marines joked when I did this the first time, "You don't want to get that cock of yours ripped off at the root, do you? Pay attention, and keep up!"

By the time we turned into a room my cock was hurting – really aching, from the incessant tugging of the marine. The effect of his strong fingers wrapped around it had had an effect, too – I was now erect, and my cock was jutting out proudly in front of me.

"Dirty fucker, isn't he?" one marine said to the other. "You wouldn't expect a prisoner to get turned on by being escorted, would you? I guess he's just a fag!" He held up his hands to his face for a moment, and went on "And smell this – he's got shit all over his cock! You'd have thought he'd have washed himself after he'd fucked that other guy, wouldn't you? Some guys just don't have any sense of how to behave in the bedroom."

I went to tell him that it wasn't my fault – Dave had called them in to the room almost as soon as I'd pulled out of him, as you know, and I hadn't had time to clean up. But as I went to speak, the marine pulled back his arm and struck me a blow across the side of my face. I went reeling backwards, and fell over, hurting my ass as I fell. Fortunately, he'd let go of my cock as he struck – I can't imagine what would have happened to me otherwise.

"Prisoners don't speak unless they're spoken to!" he snapped. "Keep that filthy mouth of yours shut unless your betters ask you a question."

The room we were in was some sort of prison or holding area – there were a number of steel-barred cells along one wall. The first marine went to open one of these, but the second – who I now saw was clearly in charge – he was not only slightly older and rather bigger – said "No – he's really pissed off the commander – we'd better cage him, in case they come to inspect him late."

"Right, Sarge."

As I looked at the older guy, I now noticed that woven into the fabric of his singlet, on one of the shoulder pieces, were three small stripes. I started to think of the younger guy as "the marine," and the older one as "the sergeant," and, indeed, all the time I was there I never got to find out their names. So this is how I will refer to them from now on.

The sergeant put his hand on my shoulder and I felt his strong fingers digging into my neck muscles. He led me further into the room, and there on the floor was a cage – literally that, a cage, such as you might keep a large wild animal in. It was made of steel bars entirely, about four feet long, three feet wide, and three feet high. It stood on its own little legs, about a foot off the ground.

The marine went over to the cage and lifted the lid, which was hinged to one side.

"Get in!" the sergeant told me, pushing me forward.

I looked at him almost blankly. I didn't really understand, I suppose, what it was I was to do. It just didn't occur to me that a man could be caged in something as small as that.

The sergeant simply kicked at my ankle with his leather combat booted foot, and I howled with pain and almost hopped around as I tried to rub myself to ease the ache.

"Get the fuck in, before I hurt you some more!" the sergeant snapped, and I realised that Dave's injunction to them not to cause physical damage to me might not apply here – presumably they could always say that I became violent, and any marks on me were as a result of necessary force.

I put one foot in the cage, and then swung the other over to join it, and stood there inside the little enclosure. It was difficult to stand, as the bars making up the floor pushed up into my soles.

"Sit down!"

The cage was so small that the only way I could do this was to push my back against one end and raise my knees up almost to my chest. The bars pressed into my back, and my toes were stubbed up against the far side of the cage.

The marine then began to lower the cage lid, and I had to bend my body and lower my head. He pushed down harder on the lid, and I heard a "snap" as the latch closed and the lid became immobile. I was really cramped – my face was looking down at my dick and my head was almost squashed up against my knees. The bars pressed unpleasantly into my ass and my back.

"He's well hung, isn't he?" The marine said conversationally to the sergeant. "When you see him in front of you he looks good, but like this you can really appreciate how low-hanging his balls are, and the size of them.

As he was speaking he reached into the cage and cupped my balls in his hand – my balls were of course hanging down between my thighs, and with my legs bent and cramped, they were totally exposed. The marines hands went through the bars easily, and there was nothing I could do to stop him – I was so crushed up in the cage that there was no way I could reach down and stop him.

He first "weighed" my balls, moving his hand up and down with them nestling in his hot sweaty palm, as if he was seeing how much they weighed. Then, still holding them closely, his fingers probed at them, separating each ball in turn, and rolling it around in my sac. You know how it is when you do this yourself, when you're testing for testicular cancer – you're oh so careful to do it softly and gently, feeling every slight twinge from the ball as you examine its shape for presence of a growth. When another man does this, there's none of that feedback, and I sat there in dread, hoping that he wouldn't get too rough or do something that would really hurt.

"A really great set!" he commented to the sergeant. "I bet he shoots huge loads when he's been milked – come and feel the size of these babies."

"No – come on, let's get out. Our shift is over, and I've got a couple of guys coming to my quarters this evening for a bit of fun and relaxation. Stop playing with the prisoner – I want to get back."

The marine let go of my balls, and I inwardly breather a sigh of relief. Without saying another word, the marines turned and walked out of the room, turning the light off as they did so. When the door was shut it was pitch black, as there were no windows, just the faint rumble of the air conditioning.

"Hey... Hey... Stop... " I shouted. But there was no response. The room sounded "dead," so I guessed it must be heavily sound proofed. I was desperate to plead with them not to leave me like this. I'm a big guy, as you know, and I was totally uncomfortable crammed into this tiny cage. As well as the ache where the bars were pressing into my body, I was already beginning to feel twinges of cramp because my muscles wanted to move. And I needed to piss – my cock was quite hard, and I had that feeling that my bladder wanted to let go.

It was evident that no one was going to come, however, and my position got worse and worse. I tried shuffling slightly, and this gave a little relief to some bits of my body, but soon the ache of the bars pressing into me started again. And all the time the dreadful cramp, and the unbearable ache from my bladder that was getting fuller and fuller as time went on. Finally, I could bear it no more – I just had to piss, and let the shot stream of urine simply fall through the bars of the base of the cage onto the concrete floor – I was glad the cage was on little legs, as I'd have been sitting there in a pool of my piss otherwise. As it was, the smell of it simply assailed me as it began to dry on the floor, and I had to sit surrounded by the stench of my own piss.

I don't know how long I was there – I think it was all night, as I had drifted in and out of sleep. It didn't matter how I tried, there was no way I could get comfortable and my muscles were in agony from the pressure of the bars, and the cramp. It was hell. I didn't know how long I could survive like this, but there was absolutely nothing I could do about it. I was psychologically very low – it was bad enough being imprisoned initially, then brought here to be "trained"; my humiliating treatment, my rape, were bad, but this was, if anything, worse. I'd been reduced to the state of a mere animal, something just to be locked in a cage and left until it was needed again.

The door did open eventually, and my eyes stung as the room was flooded with light. The sergeant and the marine were standing there, looking at me.

"Filthy animal, isn't he?" The marine said to the sergeant. "Smell that! He's pissed all over the floor. Shall I get him out and make him clean it up with his tongue?"

"You could, but we've been told to take him to the commander – there's just time for a quick fuck if we want, but not time to do that and the clean up."

"Let's fuck him then, shall we Sarge? You want to go first?"

"No – I went first last time, so it's my turn for sloppy seconds. Don't let any of the other guys know I'm going stupid in my old age, though, turning down first chance to fuck a stud like this in favour of one of the guys in my platoon! You'd best get on with it quickly, though."

"Hey, Sarge, how about turning the cage upside down, and I'll fuck him through the bars whilst he's locked rigid in there?"

"Just cut the crap, get him out, and fuck him normally. You wouldn't enjoy it, even if we did turn the cage over – his hole is so far from the bars that you'd only be able to get your cock head in, even with a big tool like yours, and if you're like me, you like to really ram it all home."

I sat there listening to all of this – they were going to fuck me again, and the thought of being fucked when I was caged and constricted was awful – I'd have no chance to defend myself, or even to try and make them stop if it was hurting. I looked out through the bars and the marine and the sergeant were both stripping for action – they untucked their combat pants from the tops of their boots, then hopped around awkwardly as they pulled them off whilst leaving their boots on. Their khaki jock straps were just tossed aside, but both men left their singlets on: they both had such muscular butts that they ledged on them at the back, and their eerect cocks stood out proudly at the front, with just the hem of the singlet resting lightly on the shaft.

The marine came over and manipulated the catch holding the lid down, and the next moment I was almost free – I could sit upright. I began to massage my neck muscles, seriously cramped from where I had been bent double. The lid of the cage was swung closed and, I thought, at least I'm not going to be put back in there.

"Up and out of there!" the marine snapped. But I found I could hardly move, I was so stiff after being constricted for such a long time. He was about to shout again, but the sergeant came over and told him to grab one arm. The sergeant took the other, and they half pulled, half hauled me up into a semi-standing position. They helped me out, and I stood feeling the bare concrete of the floor – it was such a relief after the pressure of the cage bars. I rubbed myself gingerly, running my hands down my back and over my ass, and I could feel little depressions in my muscles where the bars had pressed in on me. It hurt! I went to stretch, and tried to loosen up, and it was painful.

"Right, boy, bend from the waist. Grab hold of the cage to steady yourself...," the marine told me. "I'm going to take you standing up."

He was standing there in front of me, and I knew these two men between them could force me to do anything they wanted. But I was determined to prevent them from raping me again – I'd got nothing left to lose, after all, as I was going to be punished for turning the tables on Dave. But could I overpower them? No, I thought. I needed to try something else.

I moved towards the marine, and before he could react and stop me, I pushed my body against his, put one hand behind his head and pulled him close to me and kissed him. At the same time, I reached down and grabbed his cock and balls. I stroked him as I kissed him, then broke away and moved my head down his chest so that I could nuzzle and nip his tits. I felt his cock straining and jerking in my hands as I did this – like so many men, there was a direct line between his tits and his cock.

I carried on stroking him and teasing his balls, and he was incapable of stopping me – he was moaning and giving little cries of pleasure as I worked away at him. He was so carried away that he failed to notice that I was moving him backwards, until he was standing with his legs pressed against one of the short sides of the cage.

Now I had him! Before he could react, I pushed him so he fell backwards onto the barred lid of the cage, allowing my body to topple on to him and knock the wind out of him for a moment. Whilst he was trying to recover, I picked up his booted feet, put them around my neck, then surged forward so that my cock speared his hole.

He was struggling feebly now, recovering his breath and realising what was happening...

"No...," he started to shout. "Sarge..."

I thought that at any minute the sergeant would come and kick me, or drag me off, but I heard him laughing softly in the background.

I pushed harder, and my cock head was inside him. It was not a pleasant experience – he was dry and not stretched, and it was a huge effort to push my cock home. If I hadn't been absolutely rock hard and intent on what I was doing, it couldn't have happened. He screamed now as I slammed forward with all my might, impaling him on the full length of my cock. Without lube, it must have been hurting him like hell.

He tried, feebly, to chop at my neck with his boots, but I pushed them off my shoulders and started to thrust – hard – in and out of him. I reached down and grabbed each of his nipples, taking them between the nails of my thumb and forefinger and pushing my digits together so that my nails dug into his sensitive flesh. He started to scream – I don't know whether it was from the fucking or the nipple play. The feeling of power was fantastic – I'd gone from being a caged animal to a man, a man who was taking what he wanted from another, with no concern for the feelings of that man.

I carried on fucking, revelling in the marine's cries and the "slap, slap, slap" noise as my pubic area smashed into his sensitive bare ass. I wanted it to go on for ever. But my own body took over, and, probably a a result of the astonishing exhilaration I'd got from taking a man like this, I simply shot my load. I had to stop then as, as you know, it hurts me to carry on jerking off or fucking once I've cum.

I pulled out of him, quite roughly, and stood there looking down on my victim – his head was back, his eyes were closed, and he was groaning. The smell of his shit coating my cock rose to my nostrils, and when I looked down I could see my cock shining with the combination of his crap and my cum. Even as I watched, a small remaining snaggle of cum came out of my cock head, drooled down for a moment, and fell to the floor. My chest was heaving from the effort, my body was covered in sweat, and I felt amazing: it was the best fuck I'd ever had. I revelled not only in the feeling of sexual relief, but in the power I had to do what I wanted, what I needed to do: I had bent this marine to my will, and vanquished him.

The sergeant was looking at me, and I wondered why he hadn't intervened.

"Interesting," he finally said. "Not many of the men we get through here are tops, an especially not aggressive tops. Most of them bottom, so they lie there and take it. I wanted to see if you'd go through with it – and that marine needed a good fucking anyway – he was getting a bit above himself."

"But it can't go on, you know. You are here to be trained as a toy, and toys are there to be played with. Most masters are tops, so you've got to learn to take it. And, anyway, I need my morning fuck. So... As you were told to do before, bend over and hold onto the cage to steady yourself, and get ready to take it!"

I looked at the sergeant, and wondered if I could overpower him. The marine had got to his feet now and was coming towards me looking really pissed off. He came at me, fists raised, but the sergeant shouted "Stop! Don't damage him, or we'll both be for it!"

There was no way I could overcome both men, though – they knew it. And I knew it. But I was not going top be used passively, without a fight. All three of us stood there, cocks hanging free, and breathing hard. The only advantage the marines had were their big tough boots, and, I suppose, their training in fighting. They came at me, and were clearly used to working as a pair, though, as one of them kicked at my legs whilst the other charged my body – I fell backwards onto the floor, and the marine threw himself on to me, knocking the wind out of me as I had done him earlier.

He moved around so that he was lying across me at right angles – his heaving chest and pumping heart were close to mine, and the sergeant knelt and picked up my legs, positioning himself to start to fuck me.

He toyed with me for a few moments, sliding his hot cock head up and down the delicate areas around my ass, then said "Right – you fucked my marine dry, get ready for the same! Here goes..."

Just as he was about to thrust into me, the door opened and Dave came in. I saw him take in the scent in the room at a glance. He strode over to stand close, and looked down at the sergeant .

"Sir!" I heard the sergeant say. "Permission to continue?"

"No, sergeant! That cock of yours will tear him if you go in like that."

"But sir, we want to punish him. He fucked the marine dry, and he needs to be taught a lesson..."

"No, sergeant. He's got to be punished anyway, for yesterday. But he's only here for a couple more weeks, an we can't risk his anus being torn or damaged – that wouldn't make much of a gift from the people of the USA to our Arab friends, would it?"

"Fuck him by all means, and fuck him hard and brutally if you want – I don't even mind if you tenderise his rump a bit first, but you must lube him."

Well, what can I tell you? Whilst the marine lay across me holding me down, the sergeant quickly and efficiently jerked me off – one of his big fingers was pushed up my ass and I felt him probing for my prostate... And then I shot immediately.

He slicked his cock with my cum, and even poked a finger up me once or twice to spread more of my cum around, and then he fucked me – hard, very hard. And it hurt – even though he could slide in and out, I wasn't relaxed and I tried to resist him. The big man grunted with the effort and really had to use all his strength to get inside me, then he simply slammed away, with no concern for me at all – he just wanted something warm and moist to get him off. As I lay there with him pistoning in and out of me, with the other naked marine holding me down still, I was almost in despair. It wasn't so much the pain, as the humiliation.

Dave just stood there watching – not so much watching the sergeant, as looking at my face. I tried not to shout or scream with the hurt I was feeling, but kept up a bitter stream of invective at the way I was being used.

"We've still got a long way to go," Dave observed. "Most men soon take to proper sex, once they have been introduced to it, but this one seems to have something odd about him. Most men I know would love to have two superb marine bodies playing with him. How odd!"

Part 8

All that morning as I went through my programme of forced exercises, and all the afternoon when I was again doing the assault course with the marines in training, I was wondering what was going to happen to me – what punishment would Dave have for me?

The marine and the sergeant took me from the assault course and watched as I thoroughly scrubbed myself down under the showers, then led me off into Dave's room.

"It's bad news for all of us," he began, looking at the two marines. "The State Department has said that under no circumstances can Steve be harmed. So the three of us are going to be deprived of a lot of fun. And they were specially keen to emphasise that NOTHING was to happen to him – so you can't even work him over!"

My spirits began to rise. It's not that I'm physically afraid of what they might do to me, but, after all, it's only human to be worried, isn't it?

"However," Dave Continued, "They were interested to hear about his role as an aggressive top, once I had related the incidents between him and me, and what happened when he was uncaged yesterday. We're supposed to find out exactly how strongly he takes that role – we know it is possible to fuck him, but will he fuck "on demand" or does he have some silly scruples? If he's a true top, he'll fuck anything that he fancies, whenever he can, and I've been asked to test him."

"Sir," the sergeant suggested, "We have the new intake of recruits at the moment. They're almost all virgins, and perhaps we could use the prisoner to kill two birds with one stone, so to speak... Get some of the new recruits used to real life in the marines, and test the prisoner."

"A great idea, sergeant. Let's go and select a few candidates..."

They motioned me to go with them, and the sergeant, the marine, Dave and I went through the complex. We ended up on a balcony overlooking a giant gymnasium, and there were about 30 young guys – none older than 20 or so, I would guess – being put through their paces by a drill sergeant.

"These recruits are the ones we take who don't go to college," the sergeant was explaining to Dave. "As you know, this base trains for very special overseas duties – guarding embassies, and so on. There are only a few marines at each place, and so they need to get on well together – fraternisation with the local population is not usually allowed, and so they need to find their sexual relief with their fellows. Unless, of course, some big Washington politician is passing through and asks the ambassador to find him a little relaxation for the night, in which case they do have to perform that service, too. So we select guys who aren't married, and being as they've passed the basic tests for entry into the marines, they've all got reasonable bodies anyway. But we generally have to teach them about sex – most of them have just fucked around with girls at high school, and need a proper education. We haven't started that part of their training yet, though, as this batch only arrived yesterday."

As we stood there watching, the drill sergeant blew his whistle and the young men formed up into a neat line standing at attention. The sergeant dismissed them, and they jogged out through the gym doors. We crossed to the other side of our balcony and we could then overlook the changing room – the men were all stripping off their Ts and shorts, and making their way towards the communal showers.

Dave and the sergeant were discussing the scene below, and then began to point at some of the men. Their debate went on for a few minutes, during which time the men finished showering and towelling themselves dry, then dressing in their marine uniforms. The sergeant left the balcony and appeared in the changing room, and spoke to three of them, who then followed him out.

"Right!" Dave then said. "Off we go..."

We walked back through the complex to the room where I was being kept, and outside the door Dave told me what I was to do.

"Inside is one of the three marines I chose for you. Go in there, and fuck him. He's a virgin. You can be as rough or as gentle as you like, but you've got to shoot up inside him, OK?"

"No! It's not fucking OK! I'm not going to rape a guy, just to please you."

"Don't be so stupid! Look, Steve, if it turns out that you are a top and you enjoy fucking men, rather than just being fucked, you'll have a much easier life of it. Your new master will treat you a lot better, and you'll have a lot more fun. Personally, I don't care what happens to you, so you won't be doing it to please me, you'll be doing it to make a better life for yourself. I've made it easy for you, too – I've chosen a really great looking man to get you started – they were all quite good looking and quite turned me on, but I noticed this one had a nice bubble butt, and he really looks fuckable. And don't worry about you raping him – all these guys are going to lose their virginity in the next day or so – you heard the sergeant explaining about how they have to learn to satisfy their own sexual needs with their colleagues, didn't you? Well, how do you think that all gets started – it's part of the training here to get the more experienced marines to teach these recruits all about sex."

"Look, I don't think..."

"Steve, you no longer think. You do as you're told. I know you can fuck – and I think you like it. I thought you were fucking me as a punishment when you started, but for your own enjoyment by the time you finished. Well, do the same now. And, if it makes you any better, think about the recruit – you could be really gentle on him, whereas the sergeant, or one of the other marines, could be quite brutal..."

I knew he was right, of course – even as he was talking about fucking a recruit I felt myself start to go hard. I'd tried to stop it, tried to think about something else, but it didn't work – I now had an erection, and Dave could plainly see it. I really had enjoyed taking Dave, and I'd seen the three marines he'd picked out of the changing room, and all of them did excite me a bit, although I wasn't sure I'd want to fuck a 19 year old.

"I'll give you 30 minutes," Dave said. "You can do what you like – chat to him, cry in the corner... But after 30 minutes I'll come in and look at the guy's ass. If your sperm isn't leaking out of it I'll consider you a failure and just tell my bosses that you're not a top. So get in there!"

I opened the door and went in. The recruit looked very surprised – I guessed he was about 19 as they'd said, but he was very mature. He started in surprise when he saw my naked body.

"They've told you about sex, haven't they?" I had decided to be bold, and to see what happened.

"Yes... Sir. When you accept an assignment to this special unit they make it pretty clear you've got to learn to have sex with other guys."

"Good. So get out of that uniform, and let's get started."

He looked a bit startled – I suppose he hadn't thought it would be so soon, or with a guy like me! He might have thought he was going to just play with his fellow recruits. But he sat on the edge of the bed and unlaced his boots and took them off, then pulled his socks off. Standing up, he unbuckled his belt and let his combat pants fall to the floor, so he was standing there in his khaki T-shirt and boxers.

"Come on, boy... If I'm going to fuck you, you need to get naked."

"Uh... Sir... I don't think anyone said anyone said anything about fucking – I only fuck women, sir. I thought sex with the other guys was about jerking off..."

"I don't care whether you fuck women, or sheep, or goats! It's me who is going to do the fucking here, not you, and it's your ass I'm interested in. And I don't care what you thought, about jerking off... I'm telling you that you're going to be fucked. You're going to feel this hot cock off mine up that virgin ass of yours. Now, we can either do it with your co-operation, in which case I think you'll enjoy it, or we can do it without, when you'll find it a lot tougher."

"Sir... I don't..."

"Shut the fuck up! Get naked now, or else! Can't you see my cock's ready?" I had by now got a hard erection, and my cock was sticking out rigidly in front of me.

He stood there, not sure of what to do. So I took control. l and pushed him so that he fell back on to the bed, with a surprised look on his face. As he did so I grabbed the elastic waistband of his boxers and stripped them off him, and before he could react further pushed the front of his T up and flipped it over his head so that his chest was exposed but the material of the T was behind his neck still.

He had quite a good body for a 19 year old. As I stood at the foot of the bed between his legs, I saw that he still needed to put on some muscle, but I guessed he was an athlete at school as he had no fat on him. He had a little straggle of hair on his chest, and a thin trail led down to his pubes which were a shade darker than his sandy hair. His cock was in proportion to the rest of him, and I was amused to see that he wasn't erect – obviously this scene didn't turn him on!

I'd never fucked a virgin before, especially a young guy like this, and so I decided to be as gentle as I could even though I was conscious of my time running out. I reached for the lube that was in the bedside cabinet, then turned him over on to his belly and pulled him a bit down the bed so that his ass was overhanging the end. I lubed up a finger, then reached down and started to feel for his ass, at the same time pushing down on his neck to stop him getting up.

He was muttering "No... ", so I told him to shut up and reached around until I found his cock. Evidently my finger in his hole, with the lube, had done something for him as he was now erect, so I decided to give him a double treat: I put some more lube all over my hand, and started to jerk him off. His little cries of "No" turned into sighs of pleasure, but I didn't let him cum and returned to massaging his hole, all the time maintaining my hold on his neck – it wasn't so much that I was actually holding him down, but that the pressure of my big hand on his neck was exerting a psychological pressure on him to remain there.

Time was passing, however, so I lubed my cock, forced his ass cheeks apart with my hand, and positioned my cock head at his hole, ready for entry. I loved the feeling heat radiating from his tender tissue that excited my piss slit, and the excitement of waiting to enter where no man had been before was almost overpowering. I pushed forward ever so gently, and the lad moaned into the bed. He was resisting – well, as we all know the first centimetre or so is always difficult, but I thought that the was deliberately trying to keep me out. So I simply thrust with all my might, and was rewarded with that lovely rubbery snapping feeling as my cock head forced its way in, and a little cry from the kid. I pushed further in, slowly so as not to alarm or hurt him, and the kid let out a long low moan, which was repeated as I pulled back.

The problem with long, slow fucking is of course that it's a great experience for the guy being fucked, and it's really nice to do it when you like the guy and you've got lots of time, but it doesn't take you very far towards shooting your load – I can slide in and out of a guy's ass for hours, and never cum. So after two or three strokes, I had to speed up and thrust a lot harder, and he started to shout in time with my strokes – not anything recognisable, more noises of pain and fear. Still, there was nothing I could do about that – I thrust ever more hard and violently, almost pulling out totally and then slamming the whole length of my cock into him. He was making so much noise now that I thought of pushing his head down into the mattress, but, what the hell, what did I care if everyone heard?

My excitement mounted as I fucked away, and, to tell you the truth, the kid's cries added to my pleasure. I felt that tight feeling in my balls as I prepared to shoot, and the pleasure from my cock reached a climax. I shouted as I pumped his ass full of my sperm, then collapsed forward on to him, breathing hard.

I suppose I felt a bit sorry for the kid – he was half crying now, so I lowered my voice and whispered "Hey, it's OK. It's all over. Now you're a real man."

"It's always the worst the first time," I went on, "As you don't know what to expect. But I lubed and stretched you, so there's no damage to your asshole – although you may be a bit sore tomorrow. I wanted you to enjoy it so I started gently, but I'm sorry I had to speed up as I needed to shoot. Next time, find a guy who's got the evening to spare, and see what fun it is!"

Dave came in at that point, and the kid vainly tried to cover himself – I think he was a bit ashamed of what had happened. I think Dave was unnecessarily humiliating to the kid – he made him lie back on the bed, then probed his ass to make sure it was slicked with my cum. The kid would, I think, have objected, but the sergeant accompanied Dave and could clearly have ordered the young marine recruit to comply.

He wouldn't shake my hand, either, and just struggled back into his clothes whilst I went into the bathroom to wash my cock – it was covered in the kid's crap. I think he should have come with me and wiped away some of the stuff from his ass, but perhaps he was too embarrassed at staying naked any longer. Or perhaps he didn't know that's what guys do after sex – clean each other up: I'd have been happy to wipe my cum and his ass juices from around his hole for him if he didn't want to do it for himself.

When I went back into the room the kid was gone, and Dave told me I had to fuck another one in a few minutes – he was giving me 30 minutes to do it, and 30 minutes recovery time (Which, unless you're 16 years old and in your prime, isn't really enough!).

I absolutely did not fancy recruit number two. He was one of those thin, verging on weedy, guys with very bony asses and very tiny nipples. There's no way I'd have fucked him if he wasn't part of the test. When I told him what I was going to do, as I had for number one, he just shrugged and stripped off his uniform. So then I had to make sure I could summon up enough enthusiasm to get an erection, and then to remain hard long enough to get up his ass.

It isn't easy, I'll tell you, to make yourself fuck a young guy you find so uninteresting. I did my best, though, to make it OK for him, spending time to lube him and stretch him. But he just didn't react – he just lay there as if he was a piece of dead meat and never made a sound. It was really tough to force my way in to him, and I hated the way his bony ass kept pressing my pubic area – it made it unpleasant to thrust as hard as I needed to if I was to shoot. After a few minutes thrusting away desperately, with the kid giving me no encouragement by crying out, or even bucking around, I knew there was no way I could shoot. Given the short time between my last effort, the kid's undesirability, and the fact that I couldn't slam as hard as I wanted to, it just wasn't working for me. So I pulled out completely and just stood there jerking myself off frantically – that clock was ticking all the time.

Very fortunately, by squeezing my cock hard so that my flange was treated almost roughly as my thumb and fingers hit it as I jerked, I managed to stimulate myself to start to shoot – but nothing like the load I had the first time. I was careful to catch all of it, then used my finger to push it up the kid's hole. I only just got done as Dave reappeared, and he immediately went and did his inspection.

"Get out of here," he commanded the marine recruit, and to me, "Two down, one to go. But I think the last one is going to be a problem for you – he's physically a lot stronger than the first two, and no one told him about the unusual selection criteria for this marine regiment! So he's not even expecting you to fuck him – and, talking to him, it seems he only joined up in order to get away from rather a lot of ladies in his home town who he had made promises to in order to get into their pants!"

Frankly, I didn't care any longer. I was tired out, and I'd hated fucking the second kid, who hadn't turned me on at all. So if I failed, and if that meant I'd have a tougher life in future, so what? It could hardly be worse than having to "prove" myself by fucking men I didn't like.

Dave left me as I started to wash my cock and rub a towel over my sweat-soaked body – there wasn't really time for a proper shower. Just as I finished, the door opened and the third recruit came in – and something inside me flipped. All of a sudden I was no longer tired, and no longer worried about whether I could fuck him or not – I wanted my cock up this guy, I wanted to possess him – no, I needed to possess him!

What can I say about him – he was tall and muscular, and had a certain air of power about him even for a guy who was at most 20. In fact, he reminded me very much of myself as I had been less than 10 years ago. His shoulders and biceps bulged pleasantly out of his T, and his combat pants were tight enough to be able to make out the outline of a muscular butt, carried high, and, up front, a most impressive package. He had an air of glowing with good health and wholesomeness, and he was the most desirable man I've ever seen (not that I'd really been desiring men much in the past, of course!).

He looked at me standing there, holding a towel in one hand but making no attempt to cover my erect cock with it, and gave a little start. He went to go back out through the door, presumably thinking he'd come into the wrong room, but there was no door handle, as we know.

"Sorry, sir, I've disturbed you... How do I get out of here?"

"No, you haven't disturbed me. There's only one way to of here, and that requires you to get naked and take my cock up your ass. Then, and only then, can you leave."

He looked astonished. "Sir, I think there's something wrong... I was told to report for a special inspection and exercise..."

"That's right! I'm going to inspect your ass, then exercise you as you get fucked. Now, let's stop wasting time and get on with it. Strip!"

"No! You might want to walk around naked with a hard-on, but I don't do that."

"I said 'Strip!' Now, do it, before I make you."

The kid reacted by dropping into a fighting half-crouch, with his fists up. So I had a fight on my hands, obviously. I had the best part of 30 pounds in him, and I'd been practising with the marines for days now. But he was younger, and looked as if he'd done some fighting before. Plus, of course, those marine boots – a few well aimed blows at my balls, and I'd be out of it!

Foolishly he didn't start to attack me with his fists and boots, where he might have stood a chance, but instead tried one of those flashy "drop kicks" that you see all the Chinese street fighters doing on the movies. He soon discovered that real life isn't like the movies – one thing I had been taught here was good defensive moves, and as his boots came flying towards me I half turned and pulled at them, using his own momentum to direct him towards one of the walls.

He hit with a "crunch," and I threw myself on top of him. Now we were on the floor and his speed and his boots were not so much of a problem, my greater weight and strength and the marine training I'd had began to pay off. In between wrestling him, I managed to undo the kid's belt and fly buttons, and soon he was hampered by his combat pants around his knees. It was then relatively easy to get a hand inside his jockstrap, and as my fingers closed around his balls the fight was effectively over.

I had to give a couple of exploratory pulls and squeezes – accompanied by great howls from him – before he got the message that I was in control! I kicked at him with my legs and shuffled him around so that his back was lying mostly against my front, and hissed in his ear "Right, soldier. Calm down. Lie still. If you move suddenly, I'll tear your balls off. OK?"

"Fuck you – let of my balls, pervert..."

I had to give them a little twist to emphasise my point, and he shut up as soon as he could stop squealing.

"OK, soldier. Now we understand who's in control, reach down and unlace your boots and pull them off. And your socks. Any false moves, and I'll pull your balls again."

He was sweating hard already – his balls felt hot and almost slimy in my hand, his ass was almost on fire where it pressed against my belly, and there was that animal, male smell assailing my nostrils from all over his body. I think he got the message, though, as he fiddled around and then there was a double "clunk" as both boots hit the floor.

He was breathing so hard that I thought he might try something, but before I could do so I whispered "Now get out of those pants – push them off your legs." I find that lowering your voice and sounding calm, even when your heart is racing as mine was, starts to exert your control better than if you shout and rage at the guy.

Once his pants were clear of his feet I moved quickly and, still gripping his balls in one hand, used the other to pull his jock strap down and over his feet. Now he was exposed to me where it mattered, and my cock stabbed at his ass.

"No...," he shouted, and went to move away before a tightening of my grip on his balls caused him to stop.

I could have fucked him just like that, but I knew I had lots of time and wanted to experience more of his body. So I pushed him away from me and backwards onto the floor. Still holding his balls tightly, I told him to pull his T up and over his head so that it remained around his shoulders but his chest was bare. He did this, and then I went into action.

So quickly that he had no time to react, I thrust my head at his chest and clamped my mouth over one of his large, tender nipples. I started to nuzzle it and interspersed this with the occasional nip from my teeth. He reached up and tried to pull my head away, but a squeeze on the balls made him stop that. I didn't mind as his legs thrashed around in some sort of ecstasy and his voice began to scream "Stop it! No! Fucking Stop It! NO! OH! OH!..."

That magic line connecting the nips of most guys with the sex centre in their brain and their cocks had come into action. He could hardly control what he was saying, and my hand felt his cock begin to stiffen and erect. Quick as a flash, I moved my head to his other nipple, and did the same nuzzling and nipping. He was in an almost uncontrollable state now – his legs were thrashing, he was smashing the palm of one hand up and down on the floor, and his cries and shouts were verging on the hysterical. His cock was rock hard, and as it brushed against my forearm as I continued to grip his balls, I could feel the slime of his pre-cum as it covered my skin.

The more I moved my head from one nip to the other and back again the more he struggled and thrashed, and the more pre-cum flowed out from his cock head. Whilst he was in this semi-helpless state I used my other hand to start to jerk him off, and his whole attitude changed – I don't suppose he'd ever had another guy's hard hands wrapped around his shaft before, and his shouting changed into a kind of determined grunting. I was getting excited, too, as this kid's virgin cock felt so wonderful in my palm – the skin was soft and hot, and moved up and down easily over the underlying rock-hard flesh as I pulled his foreskin up and down (he was the only one of the three who was not circumcised yet, although the sergeant has told me that all uncut guys were "skinned," as he called it, within the first couple of weeks – apparently it made them easier to "mix in" in Arabic countries where they might be posted).

It was as if something infinitely pleasing to the touch had been stretched over a shaft of steel, and I started to do more and more extreme movements – allowing the palm of my hand to caress his exposed cock head, raking my thumb nail over his piss slit, and almost brutally moving his cock from side to side as I continued to jerk up and down. Of course this couldn't go on for long – the kid just wasn't used to this sort of extended workout for his cock, and big hot globs of his cum were soon hitting me.

I went on with my jerking off remorselessly, and the kid was wailing and pleading for me to stop – I guess he was one of those guys whose cocks are super sensitive as soon as they start to cum. In his weakened state, I could afford to let go of his balls and before he could react I flipped him over onto his belly and leapt astride him, sitting down with a quite hard crash just on his back at the waist, above his wonderful bubble butt. With my weight on him there was no way he could move, and so I could use both hands to firstly prise his ass apart and then to stick an exploratory finger, coated in his cum, up it.

His cries of sexual ecstasy now changed to ones of extreme anger, and he was foul mouthed about me and what I was doing. I didn't even bother to say anything – the erotic scent of his maleness, that special sweat that's only found in the sweat glands around the ass hole, was rising towards me and I was even more sexually aroused than I had been before. My breathing was quickening, my temperature was rising and drops of my sweat were falling off my brow onto his naked ass, my heart was pounding, and my cock hurt as it strained to get even harder. The feeling of his sweaty back pressed into the sensitive tissues of my ass was adding to my sexual arousal, and my cock, lying on the little growth of hair at the base of his spine and the top of his ass crack, was pumping pre-cum down on to him.

I just couldn't wait any longer. I desperately needed a warm, moist, tight ass around my cock. In an instant I had got off him, and before he could react I had kicked his legs apart and knelt between them. I reached under him to grab hold of his balls again, and pulled him up so that he was on his knees, whilst at the same time pushing his neck downwards with my other hand so that his ass rose into the air. As my excitement mounted, I thrust my cock forward and wriggled and moved my hips to try to position my cock head at his hole – if only I'd had a third hand, all would have been easy, but I couldn't let go of his neck or his balls.

It was as if I had new nerve endings in my cock head – a flood of messages was arriving at my brain telling me that my cock was between his cheeks, then rubbing through the hair in his crack, then finally... finally touching the moist stickiness of his cum that I had used to lube him. There was no stopping me now. I thrust forward, and felt that fantastic resistance that some guys put up when a real man is about to enter them. I pushed harder, and he seemed to resist more, and I could hear in the distance a voice shouting "No.. Please... No... Don't... Please..."

Somehow this only added to my raging excitement ,and I thrust forward more. He tried to escape, by lowering his ass, and I pulled him roughly upwards using his balls as a handle. His screaming and shouting increased but now it was unintelligible to me – not that it mattered. One mighty thrust of my hips and I was in – my flange slipped through his sphincter, and I could feel the shaft of my cock being gripped tightly by his ass muscles.

"Yes!" I roared in triumph, and pushed myself further home.

This was the best fuck I'd ever had. He was so moist, so tight, so unwilling – and, as I started to thrust backwards and forwards, he responded by trying to buck and throw me off. This only added to my pleasure, and the kid's gyrating body added whole new levels of sensation to those I was already getting.

As I thrust in and out, I lost all sense of trying to do it gently – I knew my pubic bone was slamming into his ass, as I could hear the "slap" it made each tome I made contact. This was echoed by his own shout of despair each time, which only served to increase my feeling of power and domination. I wanted to go deeper and harder, but my cock was at its limit, plunging in to its maximum each time and pulling out until I almost popped clear of his sphincter. I let go of his neck and grabbed at the rolled up T behind his neck – using this as a kind of handle, I was able to pull his upper body upwards a bit, so that just the tiniest fraction more of my cock could go inside him.

I was in a complete sexual passion. I was shouting, my body was slamming in to his ass, and now I was jerking his whole frame backwards to slap into my chest as I fucked away. I was making a lot of noise, I know, but I don't know what it was – it was some sort of primeval cry of total domination that the controlling male has given for aeons as he totally subjugates the weaker and less able members of his tribe.

But it was over all too soon. In spite of everything else, some tiny thing started to build inside me and I realised that I was going to shoot. There was absolutely no way I could slow down or stop for a moment so that the ecstasy could be prolonged – my body had taken over completely from all rational control, and I just had to pump cum up unto him. Intense sensations of joy flooded through me as I sensed the cum shoot along my cock and out into him, and I carried on thrusting even though it almost hurt to carry on after my initial load had been expelled – I've told you I can't do this when I'm jerking off, but somehow, with my senses overwhelmed by the intensity of my experience, I could do this now.

Then it was over. I let go of my hold of the T, which I'd been using almost as a handle to drag him upwards, and he collapsed onto the floor. I fell forwards onto him, and put out one arm on either side so that my body covered and enfolded his. The only movement now was his attempt to breathe against the weight of my body on his, and of my desperate panting for air as my body attempted to recover from this intense bout of energy. Sweat was pouring off me, and I almost slid off him as he too was covered in a deep layer of the body's natural lubricant.

I couldn't speak. I just lay on him, totally and completely happy. It didn't matter to me what happened next – I had demonstrated that I was in control, that I was the most powerful of the two of us, that I could take my pleasure using his body. This was what I was meant to do, this is, I knew, what a man was meant to experience, even though so few would actually do so in normal life.

The kid was recovering, too, and he just lay there. I could feel his body trying to get free of me, and he started to half moan, half cry. I could just make out, between his cries, words like "fucker" and "bastard," and I began to feel angry. Didn't he see that he'd lost, fairly and squarely, in our fight? Didn't he understand that a stronger man has the right to take what he needs from the weaker? Didn't he know that he'd been utterly dominated by me, and that I had taken my pleasure from him as I had a right to? Couldn't he see that this is what men did, and that, one day, if he worked hard to improve his strength, he too could experience the incredible satisfaction of taking the virgin ass of another man?

I pulled out from him, and got up. He continued to lie there on the floor, so I hooked a foot under his belly and flipped him over onto his back. He lay there, and covered his eyes with a forearm.

"That's the first time, kid. Just be glad it was with a guy who knew what he was doing – I've given you something to remember for the rest of your life – something with which you can compare every other guy who fucks your ass. You've lost your virginity, but it was a great fight, and a fantastic fuck – so thanks."

"Bastard..."

"Hey! Shut your fucking mouth if that's all you've got to say. How about a simple 'thanks'? Stop snivelling, and act like the man you're supposed to be! Firstly, you're supposed to be a marine, secondly you think of yourself as a fighter – you went for me, remember? And thirdly all guys sooner or later ought to learn to take a cock up their asses – how else can they appreciate how good they are themselves at fucking, whether it's men or women they stick it up. So just be grateful..."

"You didn't use a condom..."

"Of course not! This is meant to be fun for both guys, you know. I wouldn't get half the experience if my cock was covered in some sheath, and you wouldn't get to know what it's like to have a real load of man spunk trickling out of your ass. Can't you feel it now, oozing out of you and sticking to your thighs?"

He very wearily sat upright, put his elbows on his knees, and buried his head in his hands. I thought he might be about to cry. Something inside me made me feel intensely sorry for him, so I went and knelt beside him and put an arm around is shoulders.

"Hey, it's not that bad, you know."

"Yes it is. I've been fucked. I'm not a proper man any more."

"What's a proper man, kid? One who just lives his life without ever experiencing it, or one who knows and understands what it is that two men can do together? You've had a real man inside you tonight, and you should learn from that – think of how it will feel when you get your cock up another guy, and take what you want from him. Life is about pleasure, and taking a man's ass is one of the great things you can do – especially if he struggles and resists, as you did. Thanks, kid, for a great time! Learn from it, and go and do the same with your fellow marines – you're a big, strong buck, and you could almost certainly take any of that batch of new recruits I watched in the showers."

He was going to reply, when Dave came in and saw us. He commanded the young marine to get to his feet, and looked at him. He didn't even bother to run his finger up the kid's ass – I think he could see from the trickle of cum and brown ass juice running down his thighs that I'd taken him, and taken him well.

Dave looked at me, and said "So, Steve, three out of three. I suppose that makes you feel pretty good!"

"Actually, yes!"

"Well there's a little something you've forgotten – you're still under training, and our prime purpose is to teach you how to take your master's cock! Now, get showered, and wash the smell of those marines off your body – it's time I fucked you again."

He laughed as he said this, and I knew I was in for a difficult night. And it was, as soon as I was clean he pushed me back onto the bed, and I had to lie there and watch as he stripped his clothes off. He advanced on my, his hard cock swinging in front of him, and knelt astride my chest, pushing his knees down onto my shoulders.

He swung his cock with one hand so that it slapped my face, to show his contempt for me.

"Get on my cock, boy. Take your master's cock in your mouth," he commanded, and I could do nothing else, really, as I knew the marines were waiting outside. He fucked my face, hard, leaving me choking and spluttering after each time he rammed his cock home. I could hardly breathe when it was in me, as I'm sure it was so far down my throat it cut off my air.

He stopped after a few minutes, though, and I could see him towering over me, sweat pouring off him. He hadn't shot a load into my mouth, and I couldn't understand why.

"Did you like your master's cock, boy?"

I shook my head, and all he did was to laugh.

"Now for the next lesson. Get on my cock again, boy."

He'd gone half soft now, so I was a bit puzzled. But I took him limp cock in, and lay there, looking up at him.

"You've learned to take cock, Steve, but you haven't yet learned how to take another one of your master's gifts – his piss. Now as I start to piss, you swallow!"

I almost spat his cock out, and shook my head. "No... No..."

"Yes, boy. You're going to take your master's piss. Now open your fucking mouth and get on my cock. Or shall I call in the marines and have you spanked? You are going to take my piss, you know, so you may as well get used to the idea. Now... I'm not telling you again... GET ON MY COCK!"

As he said this, he moved his cock so that it was pressing my lips. Already a small drop of piss was hanging out of his piss slit, and I could taste the acrid saltiness of it.

"Get on my cock, boy, or face a spanking..."

So what could I do? I knew the marines were outside the door, waiting, so I opened my lips and Dave slid his cock in to my mouth.

"Now, boy, you know how real men piss, don't you? Once we get started it gets faster and faster. And a man doesn't like to have to try to cut himself off in mid stream. I don't want any of my piss spilled on the bed, as we're sleeping here tonight... Any spillage and you'll be spanked. And if I have to stop because you're not taking it all down, you'll be spanked twice as hard! So get ready to swallow."

As he said this, Dave's face contorted a little, and I felt something acid, foul-tasting, and warm start to flood into my mouth. I swallowed, and the liquid went down my throat, and I could feel its acidity on the tender flesh there where Dave's cock had been throat raping me only a few moments before. It went on and on – Dave pissed and pissed, and I had to swallow hard to stop any from spilling.

It's like a lot of things, actually – the anticipation was a lot worse than the actuality. Once I'd swallowed the first mouthful, all the rest was much the same. And it wasn't that awful – I didn't like the taste much, and the smell assaulted my nostrils – I suppose the vapours from the warm piss in my mouth flowed up my throat to them – but it was the humiliation of being used as a lavatory for Dave was the worst.

Once he'd finished, Dave pulled out from me but still knelt there, over me.

"I'm not finished yet, boy – get that mouth open!" He massaged his cock as some guys do to when they've finished pissing, to squeeze the last drops out of the urethra, and they fell into my mouth.

"Now clean me up – lick my cock with that tongue of yours to clean the piss off the outside where it's been immersed in that mouth of yours."

I did as I was told, licking his flaccid cock with my tongue as he used his hand to move it around in front of me.

"We'll repeat that lesson every day from now on, boy – a proper sex toy has to like taking all his master's fluids, in whatever way he chooses to give it to you. Now – it's time I fucked you properly."

Actually, he fucked me three times that night – he took me on my knees, on my back, and just casually lying by the side of me in the early morning. I felt completely and utterly used. Somehow, in spite of my training, I just wasn't learning to cope with being a sexual plaything.

Part 9

My training went on for another week – the gym and assault course during the day, and heavy fucking from Dave every night. The only variation was that occasionally Dave would invite the sergeant to fuck me, too, and once or twice the marine guard – although Dave sat there and watched us on these occasions to make sure that he fucked me, and that I did not turn the tables and top him as I had done before.

I got used to taking piss, too – even if Dave did not want to give it to me for some reason, he arranged for the sergeant and the marine to use me as a lavatory whenever they wanted. It wasn't so bad, really – all the men drank a lot of fluid as they all exercised a lot, and so their piss was quite weak. The only time I had a problem was when there had been asparagus in the canteen on the base and then both the sergeant and Dave had the vilest tasting piss imaginable – even as I leaned towards them to start taking their cocks into my mouth I could smell that dreadful stench of rotten eggs, mulched grass, and sewer odour – if you're one of the guys who is susceptible to the chemical in asparagus that makes his urine stink, you'll know what I mean.

Dave still had not forgiven me for fucking him, though, and he was always sending messages to Washington asking to be allowed to punish me – he told me about these in great detail as if he was enjoying getting me worried about my future. But Washington always said "no" as I was now too valuable a gift to be damaged. With a couple of weeks to go to the date of the presidential visit, there was a guarded "yes" to one of these messages, however, and I heard Dave in conversation on the phone as the details were worked out. Instead of being taken to the gym as usual, Dave, the sergeant and the marine appeared with a jockstrap, a T-shirt, and a pair of sweat pants, and I was told to pt them on. It was so long since my body was covered that it felt really strange to have fabric pressing against me – and my cock and balls were especially interesting as they were confined in the jockstrap. You know ow it is – if you're used to wearing a jockstrap, you're not aware of the feeling of it at all as you move around; then, when you take it off, your cock and balls bounce around as you walk and it feels totally different. Well, once you're used to being totally naked and your cock and balls adjust to being free, you cease to notice them moving and it's an odd sensation to have them confined.

As I stood here thinking this, the sergeant produced a pair of handcuffs and ordered me to stand with my hands behind my back so that he could cuff me. He then told me to follow him, and we went along the corridors of the building and out into the base road, where a car was waiting. All four of us got in, and with the marine guard driving, we sped out of the base and through the Arkansas countryside.

Dave amused himself by reaching into my sweat pants and inside the cup of my jock to fondle my cock as we drove along, and soon I had a raging hard – now infinitely worse as my cock couldn't stretch properly, confined as it was by the jockstrap. He also lifted my T, and played with my nipples, and again this increased my discomfort as my sensitive nipples seem to be directly connected to my cock!

It took us about an hour to arrive at some small town or other, and we turned off the main street into a side street and pulled up against a grungy sort of shop front, its glass replaced by boards, and whose sign said "TAT 2".

"OK, Steve. Now – when we're in here, not a word from you! If you so much as mention your name, or situation, we'll have to kill the store keeper as we can't afford to let your secret get out. And in addition, I've brought my cattle prod with me. It's a long time since I prodded you on that first day, but I don't suppose you've forgotten it, have you? So not a word – do you understand?"

"Yes, boss." Along with the mention of the cattle prod I remembered that I was supposed to refer to Dave as "boss".

We got out of the car and went in. It was a tattoo parlour. The store owner was a really ugly fat guy with long greasy hair. He was barechested, and his enormous gut hung over the waistband of his dirty jeans – he shouldn't display himself like that until he'd lost at least 30 pounds, but he was like this so that we could all see the garish tattoos that completely covered every inch of his body.

"Ah, more guys from the base," he said as he saw the sergeant and the marine. "I suppose you want that 'semper fi' motto on your arms, and one of those 'devil dog' pictures somewhere... You guys are all the same – no imagination."

"No," Dave cut in. "You will do this design, in black, inside a circle four inches in diameter, on this man's left butt. Nothing fancy – just this exact design."

As he was speaking Dave had taken a piece of paper out from a folder he was carrying, and handed it to the man who studied it. He looked at Dave rather oddly, but then just shrugged.

"Get those sweat pants off and lie on the table," he told me, and then he saw I was cuffed.

"What the...?" He began to ask, but Dave smoothly cut in

"Our mate lost a bet last night. He has to serve us all today, and we're keeping him cuffed to remind him. That's right, isn't it. Steve?"

I could see Dave toying with his cattle prod, so I just mumbled back "Yes, boss."

The marine stepped forward and pulled my sweat pants down, so I was standing just in my jock and T, and I moved over and lay on my belly on the table.

It took about two hours, I guess. In turn Dave, the sergeant and the marine all went out for coffee whilst the fat guy worked away. It stung like hell, but it wasn't anything I couldn't handle.

"Pretty extreme games you guys play, eh?" He'd asked me as he started, but Dave again cut across him with

"Part of the deal is that he doesn't speak except to acknowledge us other guys today," he told the man. "So don't expect him to talk to you. For every infraction of the rules, one hour is added to the 24 he's agreed to spend. And, yes, it is extreme games we play – a guy who looses has to agree to do anything his partners want, short of extreme mutilation!"

So for the rest of the time the man didn't speak to me, and just worked in silence listening to the endless drone of some hick country music station on the radio.

At last he pronounced it finished, and Dave came over and peered closely at my butt.

"It will bleed a bit for a day or so, so keep rubbing it occasionally with a mild antiseptic. It's pretty good, even though I say so myself," the man told Dave.

I then stood up, and the guy held a mirror for me to look at my butt. There, on my tanned flesh, was a black circle containing an America

Eagle, and the words around the edge read "A Gift From The People Of The USA." They had marked me as a gift now!

The man wanted me to lie and rest for an hour or so but Dave was impatient to get back. So they simply pulled the sweat pants off me, and told me to walk out to the car in just the jock and T. I felt so ashamed – even though I was used to being totally naked all the time on the base, somehow, even wearing a jock, I felt completely exposed out on the side street in this small town. Whilst they opened the car I kept looking around nervously, afraid that someone would come and see my named butt.

Dave noticed my unease, and laughed. "Where you're going, you'll have to get used to all kinds of people seeing you naked," he told me, "Not just other fit guys like on the base."

Dave wouldn't let me sit on the car seat for fear of damaging my tattoo whilst it was still raw and bleeding, so I had to lie across the lap of the sergeant, with my butt in the air. He soon began playing with my jock, idly snapping the straps to make me start, then moving the thick patch that normally covers your hole so that he could tickle it with his finger. All of this made me wriggle, of course, and he told me to lie still, else as I was in the ideal position for spanking, he'd punish me.

I never saw the countryside on the way back, therefore, and only knew we had reached the base when the car stopped and I heard the sentry challenging them.

When we got back to our normal room, Dave took great delight in making me walk up and down in front of the sergeant and the marine so they could admire my "gift tag" as he called it. Then he remarked that there was one other "decoration" that Washington had agreed to, and told me to go and lie on the bed.

"This is going to hurt him a bit, so I'll need your help," he told the marine. "Get up there and kneel on his arms. Take your clothes off if you want, so he can suck you, or you can take a piss, if you want him to," Then, to me, "Arms out at right angles..."

The marine didn't take up Dave's offer, but Dave manipulated him so he was behind my head, and kneeling on my outstretched arms – if he had stripped, his ass hole would have been immediately above my face. As it was, I could still anyway smell the musky scent of dried sweat and piss from his combat fatigues, they were so close to my nose.

Dave now straddled my body, sitting astride me facing the marine, his weight pressing down on to my belly.

"Washington has agreed to you being fitted with nipple rings," he told me. "They understand that they're very fashionable in the Gulf. Not the little tiny things you see gays in San Francisco wearing, but proper, heavy ones that will really drag at your tits. Each time you move there will be a little sensation in one of your nipples, and it will remind you that you're no longer a free man but someone's toy. And, as we know, you've got some sort of connection between those sensitive tits of yours and your cock – so I expect you'll have a lot more erections, too."

"We'd normally get that tattooist guy to do it," he went on, "But he was already a bit surprised by your tattoo. If I asked him to fit these heavy rings, rather than the normal small ones, he might have got even more suspicious. And, anyway, he'd have wanted to use an anaesthetic – whereas I want you to remember this. Let's just say that me doing this to you is another small part of the payback for what you did to me."

He leaned forward, and started to massage and tweak my nipples, and they reacted by jerking up hard and strong under the manipulation of his thumbs and fingers. I am indeed incredibly sensitive there, and as he rolled them around between his fingers, I tried to buck and thrust my body to throw him off and to make it stop – but the combined weight of Dave on my belly and the marine on my outstretched arms prevented it. Instead, I cried and shouted, so extreme was the pain becoming. My cock was also rock hard, and I could feel it scraping on the cloth of Dave's dress pants as he squatted there on top of me.

I shrieked when Dave pushed the sharp needle through my left nipple, and carried on shouting as he twisted it around to open up the hole he'd made a little. I could see Dave's fingers were now all red – with my blood, and he wiped them through my hair to clean them a bit before reaching into his pants pockets and getting something out. I was shouting again then as the metal ring he'd had in his pocked was threaded through the hole he'd made, and Dave snapped

"Shut the fuck up, and stop trying to squirm – this is the tricky bit, as I've got to close this ring up... All this noise is making me lose concentration!"

He used a pair of pliers to squeeze the thing he'd forced through my nipple, and then twisted and pulled slightly – my nipple was sending little bursts of agony through me as he did so.

"Good. That slips freely. No snagging." He commented to no one in particular.

I though I'd be let go then, but no – he did the same to my right nipple. And it's not true that they ay about it being able to bear it a second time – you know what to expect, and it's far, far worse! When he'd finally done, he told the marine to get off my shoulders, and ordered me to stand. As I did I became conscious for the first time of what has now become completely routine for me – the weight of the two big rings he'd fitted into my nipples, that I could feel tugging down on my nubs. I've got big, rounded pecs, so the rings hung down freely beneath my nubs and didn't really touch the flesh at all. Dave approached me, and I winced as he rolled the rings around.

"Do that every thirty minute or so," he told me. "I want them to keep running free whilst the scar tissue forms inside your nipples."

He left me alone that night – I was all by myself in the bed, and I just lay there thinking about things. I was now tattooed and ringed – and there were not the ordinary sort of small rings I'd seen guys with occasionally in the streets – there were big, heavy rings that really stretched my nips where they went through. Truly I'd been turned from being an ordinary sort of guy into some kind of fetish object – what else did they have in mind or me, I wondered.

The next morning my tits were still aching, but there was no let up in the exercise programme – I had to do all the gymnastics as usual, and now I was for the first time conscious of my tits in a way I'd never been before. The weight of the rings, and the way they flopped up and down as I moved, made me continuously aware of my body as I'd never been before – it was like when I first had my ass shaved: walking was a wholly new experience as you're never aware of the friction of the hairs in your ass crack until it's no longer there.

In the next two weeks my rigorous training continued – my body got fitter, leaner and stronger, and I got completely used to taking the cocks of the three men up my ass – frankly, it no longer bothered me much that they were using me as a convenient way of bringing themselves to climax. My nipples healed, and the only time they were really painful is when Dave or one of the two marines decided to give them a playful tweak when they were fucking me – they discovered that by jerking down on the rings suddenly my body would be caused to spasm upwards, and they enjoyed doing this just as they were about to cum – as Dave said, having the fuck toy buck underneath you was just that last little extra that he needed to drive him over the edge and really make him cum.

My final day in the training camp started just like all the others – I woke up with an erection, with Dave's cock pushing up my ass crack as he liked to sleep "spooned" into me. I went to get up and shower, but Dave ordered me onto my hands and knees, as he said he wanted to fuck that morning – this was unusual, but it did happen from time to time. As he pulled out of me and knelt there with his cock rapidly going flaccid, he said

"Well, that' the last time, Steve. We're off today – You're going to be taken to the Gulf, and given to your new master. So I want you to take particular care in the shower – shave your balls carefully, and re-do your crack so it's nice and smooth for when your new master inspects you."

"Look, you can't be serious... I've gone along with this until now, but you can't really mean that I'm going to be given away..."

"Steve, your fate was decided when you were in that prison, as we've told you. You've only been here at this facility so we can train you better, and give your body a final buffing and toning – there's no point in giving a gift, after all, unless you've spent some effort on it! And why do you think we've had you tattooed like that – it's to remind your new master of the generosity of the people of the USA every time he fucks you!"

"But don't worry," he went on. "They treat their slaves humanely over there now. The days when a guy like you would be routinely castrated, or blinded, are over. There just aren't all that many really good looking, virile white slaves, and so they command extraordinarily high prices. Your master will want to take care of you in the same way that he would take care of a thoroughbred racehorse or other expensive animal – you'll get good food, the right exercise, and be well looked after. Without the stress of having to make up your mind about things, and make your own living, I expect you'll live to a ripe old age."

"But you can't just give me away – I'm a man, not a gift! I'm a US citizen, not a slave..."

"You haven't learned, have you Steve? We can do anything we like! You've no relations to ask about you, and our men have been in and altered all the records of your trial and imprisonment- it just never happened, as far as the records are concerned. You've dropped of the face of the earth as far as anyone can ever tell, just like lots of single guys do. No one can ever trace what happened to you. And we're having a rather special method of shipping you out of the country – believe me, there will be no records, and no one will ever ask any questions!"

"And when you're there, t will be just the same thing – the ruler is an absolute ruler, so if he chooses to keep you locked up in his palace, there's not a thing anyone can do about it. No one will know, anyway, and there's no civil liberties people to go bleating to the courts. But if they did, the courts wouldn't hear them, as they never upset the ruler! No, your best bet is just to accept that you're going to have an exciting new life – actually, you know, a lot of guys might envy you!"

"Don't be so fucking stupid, boss. Who would envy me, being shipped off as some sort of sex toy..."

"Well, there are all those guys who like the idea of slavery, and who role-play masters and slaves. You're getting the chance to experience the real thing. Then there are the exhibitionists, who'd love the opportunity to parade around nude all the time, with their cocks swinging in front of them. And the men who can never get enough sex, and to whom the thought of having endless cocks up their asses would be just heaven..."

He stopped at this point, and pointed at the bathroom. "But enough of this. You don't have a choice, so stop worrying about it and go and get clean... REALLY clean, as I said."

When I came out of the bathroom Dave ran his hands all over me, as he'd done so many times before, checking that my ball sac was completely smooth. In spite of hating being fucked by him against my will, I still found myself unable to stop getting a slight erection though as he ran his hot finger down my ass crack and wiggled it around on the sensitive skin of my pucker. He wasn't pleased with the total effect, however, and went and got scissors and trimmed the length of my remaining pubic hair a bit, as he said it was getting too long. And I had to stand with my arms raised above my head, too, whilst he snipped away at the hair in my pits.

I knew something big was about to happen when Dave threw some clothes at me and told me to dress – a T shirt, some sweat pants, and trainers. It felt so strange having fabric against my skin again, and I had new sensations to contend with – the way my swollen and extended nipples with their heavy rings grated against the cotton of the T, and the odd feeling of the cloth of the sweat pants against my shaved balls and cut cock: I'd never realised how much my foreskin protected my cock head from chafing.

Dave ordered me to follow him, and the sergeant and my marine guard accompanied us to the outside of the building where we got into the back of a big official car. I was cuffed to an arm rest "just in case you get any ideas about trying to escape," as Dave said.

The car sped along the Interstate, and we seemed to be heading for Virginia. We never stopped – we had sodas to drink, and when I wanted to pee Dave said I either had to hold it, or do it in one of the empty cans – "it's not as if we all haven't seen you peeing, after all," he reminded me.

I must have dozed, as the next time I was aware of something happening was when we sped into an air base, stopping only for passes to be examined at the gates. We then had an escort which drove us out onto the base, and to my astonishment we ended up at the rear steps leading to Air Force 1! Dave uncuffed me, and he and the sergeant and the marine, taking good care that I couldn't make any fuss or disturbance, hustled me up the steps.

I'd seen pictures of the inside of the plane, but the part we went to wasn't at all like the bit you see there – no luxurious seats, no conference tables. Instead, I was bundled into a tiny cell, which Dave told me was on the plane in case there ever was a problem with any of the presidential staff, or the press corps, or the crew – they could be overpowered, and then restrained until the journey was over. There was a window in the cell, and I could watch the preparations being made for take off – the loading of supplies, and then a large group of people arriving who were evidently the press corps as they all took photographs of each other. I tried banging on the window of my cell and waving, in the hope that they would see me and that there would still be time to prevent my "export," but it was no good – a couple of reporters actually waved back, as they evidently thought I was another passenger!

It was of course a very boring flight. Dave brought me food, and under armed guard I was allowed to go to the lavatories, but was always locked back into my cell. There was absolutely no chance I could make contact with anyone else on the plane.

I never got to see the country we landed in as it was dark when the plane touched down and we taxied to a halt by a huge terminal building. I watched the presidential party, and the press, all disembark, and some time later Dave came and cuffed my hands behind my back before leading me down the steps into a limo, that drove us off into the town. I couldn't see much, but it looked pretty much like I'd imagine an Arabic town to look like – low buildings, dark, narrow streets. We finally drive in through a pair of massive gates, guarded by marines, and I saw a sign saying "Embassy Of The United States Of America" as we went through.

I tried to tell the marines who escorted me from the car that I was a US citizen being given into slavery, but one of them said "Sir, please stop that crap! We are all graduates from the training base here, the one you have just come from, and we are specially chosen to execute special missions. So shut the fuck up." As he said this, he casually reached down and squeezed my balls through the fabric of my sweat pants – not something I'd ever expect a marine to do – so I knew he wasn't bullshitting me. And I knew it would be painful if I didn't obey him.

Dave fussed over me deep in the embassy cellars where I was taken – I had to crap, shave, and take an enema to make sure I was properly clean inside. He supervised my shaving again, then rubbed a light oil all over me so that I was faintly glistening.

"My, you are handsome, Steve," he said. "You were pretty hot when you first came to us, but now, buffed, oiled, tattooed and with those rings, you're enough to cause any man's cock to want to thrust up you! The ruler sure is a lucky man to be able to use you whenever he wants."

"But let me give you a few words of advice," he went on. "Once you've been handed over, don't try to escape, or offend your new master. It's worth remembering that he's an absolute ruler here, and has the power of life and death over you. Although it would be expensive for him as you'll be a costly piece of his property, he could have you killed. What's more, if you displease him, he doesn't even have to have you killed – I've heard that unruly or troublesome guys here get dealt with in the old fashioned way."

"What's that?"

"Did you ever have a pet dog when you were a kid?"

"Well, yes."

"Do you know what veterinarians do to pet dogs if the owners think they're too frisky, or too difficult to control?"

"No"

"Well, they simply cut their balls off. And that's what they do to unruly slaves here, I'm told. They don't even have to worry about you losing your looks, either – in the olden days they'd have simply cut them off, and cauterised the wound to stop it bleeding. But with modern surgical techniques they can simply slit your sac open down the back, cut the balls out, then replace them with ones made of plastic and sew you up – You look just the same, but you're no longer a man. You'll be a whole lot calmer and better tempered without all the testosterone surging through you, but you'll know you're no longer a man."

"So fucking what! I'm no longer a man anyway, if I have to accept that I'm just some sort of fuck toy..."

"Oh for Christ's sake, Steve, don't start all that shit again! I know you thought you were straight when you started, but we soon proved to you that you actually like proper sex, didn't we – or am I mistaken in thinking that when you fucked me that was the best fuck of your life, to date? So we know you like proper sex, it's just that you haven't learned yet the pleasure of taking it from a man that's superior to you in every way – either tougher, smarter, or more powerful. You like to give it, but one day you will find there's equal pleasure in taking it – providing, as I say, the other guy totally dominates and controls you. It's human nature for a guy to resent being fucked by someone he considers less of a man, and that's why you hate being fucked by me. But just as you enjoy fucking, so one day you will find that man who will master you, and then you'll see the other side of the coin."

"Until then, just grit your teeth, or whatever – if your new master decides to have you fitted with prosthetic balls, you'll never experience the pleasure of fucking again. And I'm told that you won't even want to jerk yourself off. So get real!"

"Now," he went on, "Your new master is coming to a reception at the embassy here this evening. After he's met the president, and dined, the ambassador will bring him in and hand you over."

"Don't I even get to meet the fucking President? I could at least tell him what I think bout his 'gifts' ..."

"No, Steve – the President of course knows all about it, and authorised this whole operation. That's how important our relations with your new master are. But there's always the risk of a reporter seeing or hearing something, so just to make sure the President remains squeaky clean, he won't actually be present. It's possible that the great people of the USA wouldn't understand the necessity for doing this to you, so we don't want even the possibility of his being compromised."

Dave gave me a kind of tunic to wear – like an oversize T-shirt, that had a deep V neck, was deeply slit up the side but was only just longer than my cock when I was standing up. Somehow wearing it I felt more humiliated than when I was nude – I was deliberately being given something "sexy" to wear, and not being allowed to display my naked body as a normal man would. We then went up into a luxuriously furnished room in the Embassy, and sat and waited – or, rather, Dave sat and waited but I stood: if I sat down, the tunic thing rode up and exposed my cock and ass, and it made me feel worse, as I've said.

When the door opened, it was somehow depressingly normal – I'd expected a great set of servants and bodyguards, but there was just a guy in 'traditional' Arab dress, and a middle aged, overweight guy in a tuxedo.

Dave leapt to his feet. "Excellency, Mr Ambassador..."

The guy in the tux all but ignored Dave. Instead, he said to the Arab "Excellency, here is the gift of the people of the United States, as our President told you, a symbol of the high regard in which we hold the people of our country. This is the man you so admired on your visit to our country last year, and we have had him specially trained, and hope that he will constantly remind you of our country, the pleasant time you had there, and the things that make the American people great."

The Arab was looking at me with enormous interest. He came over, and ran his hand down my arm, pinching and testing the biceps as he went. Then he reached up and felt my jaw line, and said softly "Open your mouth".

I was kind of startled, and did as I was told, and without hesitation he poked a finger into my mouth and ran it around under my lips.

"Excellent!" he mused. "A good strong jaw. Excellent teeth. A hot, wet tongue. And sweet breath. Time to unwrap the rest of the present, I think."

Then, to me, he simply said "Get naked!"

Well, what had I got to lose? I kind of shrugged, and in one motion pullet the loose tunic over my head to stand there in front of the three of them. I decided my fate was probably inevitable, and so I might as well try to make a good impression, so I clasped my hands behind my head, moved my feet slightly apart, and thrust my chest and hips forward so I was properly "displayed".

"Excellent... Excellent...," the Arab was muttering as he expertly examined me. His cool, strong hands ran all over my pecs and my flat stomach. He moved behind me and dig his fingers into my neck muscles, feeling their power. Both hands ran down my back, then across my butt. A finger probed my ass crack, and then he cam around to the front again.

"One foot on the sofa," he commanded, and I moved over and placed one foot on the arm of one of the luxurious sofas in the room. With one leg bent almost at right angles, the Arab was then able to feel the muscles in my thigh and calf more conveniently – he was obviously an expert at these sorts of examination! And, of course, my balls were swinging freely so that when he came to examine them it was so much easier for him.

It was interesting that as he had been examining me he'd not really looked at me as his eyes were focused on the parts of my body he was feeling. But once he had my balls in his strong hand he looked directly into my eyes. They locked onto mine, as he "weighed" my balls up and down, then started to probe at them and separate them in his palm using his thumb. I think we was watching my reactions very carefully, and when he squeezed and I got a momentary twinge of pain, he seemed very satisfied. I was of course erect, and he seemed to enjoy encircling my cock with his hand and gently stroking it, again whilst looking into my eyes.

"Excellent! Forgive me, Ambassador, but when the Russians gave me a slave boy I'd admired, I found that they'd had him castrated and fitted with fake balls! So I was examining this toy here to make sure he still had feeling down there – I don't like to take men to my bed who are not real men, capable of shooting a good load of live spunk everywhere. The Russians apologised, of course, and said that they had had to do it to calm the lad down as they didn't think he's otherwise co-operate. Foolish – I'm fully experienced at taking every man I want, whether they 'co-operate' or not."

"Now, please leave us for a few moments."

The ambassador nodded, and went to leave, but Dave just stood there.

"I told you to leave," the Arab snapped.

"But sir, I'm guarding the..."

"Leave!"

The ambassador and Dave (reluctantly!) left, and the Arab came and stood in front of me.

"You can put your arms down."

I did, and stood there, with them relaxed, at my side.

The Arab came closer, and suddenly he was kissing me. His hand went around my head, and his strong tongue forced its way into my mouth. One half of me wanted to respond, but another part of me hated this violation. I raised my hands, and gently, very gently, pushed him away.

He stood there, glaring at me. "You know I could have you castrated, or killed, for defying me?"

"Yes... Master."

"Ah, so you do acknowledge that you're my master. So why do you prevent me from tasting your mouth?"

"Master... I ... Well, I do understand that I have been given to you. And I suppose that's not much worse than being in prison in the USA. But I don't like being forced to have sex..."

"I understood that you had been trained in all the arts of proper manly sex..."

"Yes, master. That man who was in here, Dave, trained me. He forced me..."

"Ah... So you've been trained, but you don't like it... Excellent! I like a man who resists..."

"No... Master... I think I do like sex with men. When I fucked Dave – actually, raped is more like it – it was absolutely the best..."

"Tell me more!"

So I related to him how I'd been trained, and how I'd taken my revenge on Dave. When it was over, he was laughing slightly.

"So, what am I to do now? I am even more entranced by your body than I was when I first saw you. And it would be rude to turn down a gift. I think we need to see just how deep your disgust is. On your knees!"

I knelt down, feeling the luxurious carpet on my legs. The Arab stood in front of me, fumbled with his robes, then pulled them apart to reveal a cock that was at least as big as mine.

"Give me the kiss of obedience, slave."

"Master... ?"

"Kiss the tip of my cock, to show that you understand that I am your master."

Actually, I don't have any problem with kissing or sucking cocks, as you know. Since arriving at the training camp I'd really begun to question why the term "cocksucker" is such an abusive one in the USA – its actually really great to have a big, hot, moist cock in your mouth, and it's one of the best things that two guys can do for each other, I'd found. So I leaned forward and gently pressed my lips to the tip of the Arab's cock. I experienced that delicious warm saltiness from his sweat, I reached out my tongue and gently lapped around his meaty flange.

"Ah, so you like cock, do you?"

"Yes, Master. It's just that... "

"Well?"

"It's just that I hate being fucked. I love the taste of cock, the feel of it, and I love another guy's body all over me. But I hate being fucked. I'm a 'top', Dave says, a natural, aggressive top, and so I like fucking. But I hate being fucked."

"A natural, aggressive top? You'll happily fuck another man, even if he doesn't want to?"

"Well, master, I don't know. But I love the feeling of an ass around my cock. And utterly dominating the other guy, to make him take me, is the most exciting thing I've ever known. And, of course, once you've done it, the other guy recognises that you're his superior and doesn't mind it anyway. It's just the anticipation of it, the thought of being fucked against your will, that's the problem. When it's happened, the other guy accepts it, and even enjoys it..."

The Arab laughed. "That's my experience exactly! You're just the sort of slave I need for a very special task... But... I think... An experiment."

He went over to the door, and called Dave in.

He sat on the sofa, and Dave stood there in front of him. "Excellency, if the toy has been troublesome..."

The Arab ignored Dave, and said to me. "Right. Show me what you're made of. Take this man for the second time!"

Dave went to say something, but I sensed the Arab was serious. And what had I got to lose? I sprang at Dave, who tried to draw his gun, but failed – he got it out of his concealed shoulder holster, but I had by this time charged him and swept him onto the floor. I banged his hand hard on the carpet, and the gun flew out and skittered into a corner.

Dave was fighting – and he was trained – but so was I now. And I was fitter and stronger. It took me a few moments, but I managed to throw myself on top of him and "wind" him, and this enabled me to undo his belt and pull his pants and boxers down to his feet. Then whilst he was still gasping for breath, I picked him up and threw him over the arm of the sofa.

I was in a frenzy now, as his ass stared up at me. I pushed his shirt up his back, forced his head down into the cushions, and simply thrust myself hard and brutally into him.

His shouts and squeals were masked by the heavy upholstery as I gave him another complete fucking, caring only for my own satisfaction. I thought I wouldn't have much time, so, even had I wanted to, there was no opportunity for a slow languorous fuck. Instead I pounded away, pulling out almost completely and slamming back in so that my pubic bone slapped against his ass muscles each time. I was so charged up with sexual energy that I only had to thrust about twelve times before I shot my load – a huge load, I though, that pumped deep up into Dave.

Then I just as quickly pulled out, and stood there in front of the Arab, the last drops of my cum falling in a thick drool from my cock and forming a little heap on the carpet.

"Very impressive!"

He went to the door, and summoned the ambassador in. To his credit, the poor man looked a little shocked as he saw Dave trying to scramble up off the arm of the sofa and pull his clothes up.

"Please convey to the President, and the American people, Mr Ambassador, our sincere thanks for these gifts. The naked toy is magnificent, and so well ornamented. But the bonus gift will cause me great pleasure, too..."

"Excellency... Bonus gift...?"

"Yes, I have decided to accept the gift of this man here, the one who trained this toy so well. I am especially grateful for the gift of two such splendid pieces of man flesh – although I have only seen the ass of the second one, so far, I am sure that he will be pleasing overall. In fact...," he turned to Dave and continued "I would like to see both of my toys together. Unclothe!"

Dave went to protest, but the Arab nodded to me and I had to use my greater strength to "help" Dave get naked.

"Excellency," the ambassador was saying as this was going on, "Whilst the American people want to be the friends of your country, we are not able to give you this second gift... This is a man in the armed forces of our country, a soldier..."

"Not able to give... Or unwilling? So much for your so-called 'friendship'. If he is a soldier, call your president and tell him to command the man to enter my service."

Dave went to say something, but the Arab said to me "Silence this slave! The noise he is making is displeasing."

So I grabbed Dave from behind, wrapped one arm around his body and pulled him tight to me so that my cock nestled in his naked ass, then wrapped my other arm around his mouth to shut him up.

The Ambassador saw that this was an argument he wasn't going to win, and bowed. "Excellency, I am sorry if there has been a misunderstanding. The American people will of course gladly give you the additional gift you request, if it will help cement relations between our two countries."

And that was it! My master allowed me to sit next to him in the limousine that took us from the Embassy to his palace, and I remember the feeling of the cold leather on my naked ass as I slid in beside him. But Dave, who had foolishly tried to protest again when the Embassy's marines were called to handle him, was unceremoniously bundled into the trunk!

My master kissed me again as the car sped through the night, and fondled my cock and balls, and of course I did not resist. And later that night, although I at first hated it, I did discover that even a top like myself can learn to enjoy being taken by a truly masterful master. My master has ultimate power and authority, and when he chooses to fuck me, I now see it for the privilege it is.

My main purpose in life is to fuck the men my master has fucked, as soon as he had finished: he has a horror of his cum being drained from a man's ass after he has used him and having it sold to a seed company – he knows that there are many women who would pay high prices for being able to fertilise themselves with the semen from such a powerful man. So I have to fuck the men immediately after him, so that no one could be sure it was his cum they were buying, and not mine! It's a bit hard on me, actually, as I hardly ever get to use a really tight, dry ass – it's always "sloppy seconds" for me. Except, of course, when I use Dave – and that's almost every night.

We are both personal servants of our master, sharing his quarters. But our master has a natural affinity to me as we are so alike, whereas he treats Dave as a more ordinary servant. My master rewards me with the use of Dave whenever I choose, providing, of course, that my cum production is not affected – but I say that "use it or lose it" is the name of the game, so I use Dave at lest once a day. I don't think he'll ever get used to being naked, either – even though my master has had the same magnificent rings added to him as Dave added to me.

It's a funny old life, isn't it? If anyone had ever told me that I'd end up living a life devoted to sex, I'd have laughed. I only wish I'd discovered proper sex earlier – all those early years of my life wasted, when I could have been fucking my school fellows and friends. Perhaps if I'd learned about proper sex earlier I'd never have ended up in prison in the first place.

About the Author

Pete Brown is a very busy man who lives in London and loves to write about how he wished he lived.